PALO DURO AMBUSH!

At first light as they saddled their horses, a clattering noise burst upon them, rocketing through the canyon.

"Ambush!" cried Wofford.

Hell, yes, that's gunfire, realized Tyrone.

Like rain, bullets drummed and pock'd the ground, stung trees and, a torrent now, flicked and churned the surface of the river behind him.

Wofford was shouting, "Cover, cover!"

Tyrone scrambled down, belly-sliding toward a hump-back rock.

The sound was like swarming bees. Buzz, buzz, buzz, buzz, *sting!*

The bullet felt like the bite of a yellowjacket, he thought as his head snapped back; a puppet's being yanked by a string. For an instant his whole body tingled. Then cold swept through, ice in his blood. His mouth tasted like metal. Numbness rose in him like the stroke of a woman with cool hands.

Limp as a rag doll, he dropped behind the rock, flat on his back on the hard canyon floor. . . .

OWLHOOT TRAIL

H. PAUL JEFFERS

ZEBRA BOOKS
KENSINGTON PUBLISHING CORP.

ZEBRA BOOKS

are published by

Kensington Publishing Corp.
475 Park Avenue South
New York, NY 10016

First printing: October, 1990

Printed in the United States of America

To Kevin Gordon

Out where the handclasp's a little stronger,
Out where the smile dwells a little longer,
That's where the West begins.

ARTHUR CHAPMAN
Out Where the West Begins

Introduction

When a pair of hardcases known as the Ludlum Boys barged through the green batwing doors of Long Charlie Carew's saloon on a sultry August night in Wichita, the steely-eyed cousins were not looking for a pair of cold beers to wet their whistles.

Every man in the smoke-filled saloon knew they'd come there gunning for a new kid in town known as Irish.

From *Showdown in Hell Town*
by Harry Tyrone

The tales which Harry Tyrone spun about the Wild West a century ago thrilled millions of readers with the exploits of the outlaw Ludlums and their nemesis, the kid called Irish; a righteous gunman of Abilene known as Morgan; the battling marshal of Wichita named Mike Meagher; a cattle rancher with the improbable name of Shanghai; and Texas Ranger Andy Wofford who tracked the rugged and treacherous High Plains of Texas in pursuit of the notorious Saldana, as murderous an outlaw as ever plagued the frontier.

How a scruffy kid who'd been honed by the whetstone of growing up on his own in the tough East River slums of New York City got to be a writer wandering the frontier and rubbing elbows with those characters is a saga that Tyrone never got around to telling himself. Yet his story is full of adventures equal to those he described in the dime novels that flourished in the brawling decades after the Civil War when America was stretching westward.

Tyrone hadn't been old enough to join in the fighting between North and South. Born in 1850, he was the son of a drunken, wife-beating seafarer who vanished forever when Tyrone was six. His mother, Maggie, was a remarkable woman who saw that her son got an education, introducing him to books and teaching him how to write. At the age of eleven he turned to supporting them, first by selling the *Herald* newspaper on the street and at the age of twelve by working as a stable boy tending to the horses that pulled the wagons that delivered the paper. At fifteen, quite by chance, he was noticed by a horse fancying newspaper reporter by the name of Ben Turner. A short, bald, cigar-chomping bundle of energy who kept track of the police blotter for James Gordon Bennett's paper, Turner was impressed by the stableboy's education, however rudimentary, and intervened with Bennett to provide the boy a better job, a move that uplifted Tyrone and provided Turner with an assistant.

The job was running errands and carrying copy from the press shack on Mulberry Street to Park Row when Ben didn't want to chance a Turner scoop being picked up by the reporters of competing papers eavesdropping on his telegraph key.

Between these excursions, the young Tyrone soon expressed an interest in learning how Turner did his job. Pleased to show him, Turner quickly discovered that the boy was quite bright and had a flair for journalism.

Soon he was permitting the boy to write lesser stories, most of which found their way into print without significant editing for style or grammar. In 1867, when Bennett's eccentric son and namesake required a police reporter for his father's second newspaper, the *Evening Telegraph,* Turner, who became the fledgling paper's city editor, recommended his protegé.

At this time, Tyrone was a short, scrappy 17-year-old who had shown himself to be capable of turning who, what, where, when and why into a snappy story with the best of the men who worked in the newspaper offices on the first and second floors of a tenement opposite the Police Headquarters on Mulberry Street. Like his elder colleagues, he whiled away the time between news stories drinking and playing cards next door in a saloon known as the Garden of Eden.

Before the war, the dives, dance halls and houses of ill repute in New York City had been confined to the notorious Five Points district and along the equally dangerous Bowery, but scarcely had the South laid down its arms at Appomattox than Seamus McGlory opened up new territory for resorts farther west. Within the very shadow of Police Headquarters located at 300 Mulberry, McGlory threw open the portal to his Garden of Eden at No. 301, laughingly declaring, "The nearer the church the closer to God."

Bearing no resemblance to a garden, the Eden was a vast smoke-filled room with paintings of voluptuous women on the walls, sawdust on the floor, chairs and tables for seven hundred customers and an O-shaped bar in the center where McGlory was a constant but restless presence with a white apron draped over a pot belly, a policeman's nightstick swinging from a thong looped around his thick wrist, a stogie at the corner of his mouth and attentive Irish eyes surveying the place and looking out for the kind of trouble that might bring the coppers across the street at a run. "The troot of it is," he warned his rowdy customers in a brogue, "that in the original Garden of Eden, it took the good Lord quite a while to catch onto the mischeeveeous t'ings that was goin' on.

But in this loovly little Eden of moine, Oy don't intend to miss nuttin'."

Like his elder colleagues, Tyrone whiled away the time between news stories at McGlory's peacefully, giving McGlory no cause for intervention, until the rainy night of April 18, 1873 when hapless Peggy Brady ran afoul of a waterfront layabout and drunken bully known only as Crazy Sid.

As best anyone could remember, nobody had ever done anything decent for Peggy—who was a harlot, after all, and not all that young or pretty—but in the wee hours of that fateful morning, Tyrone did so with deadly effect.

Although no one could say for certain just what sparked the trouble between Peg and Sid, all agreed that when Sid slapped her and knocked her down, Tyrone sprang to her assistance, fists at the ready. Then, somehow, a gun came into play and in a tug of war for its possession, Sid wound up taking a bullet clean through the head.

"None of us ever knew Crazy Sid had any brains to speak of," said McGlory, "until we seen 'em splattered on the floor!"

To the police who rushed across Mulberry to investigate, McGlory and everyone else in the Garden of Eden vowed that Tyrone had acted in an honest, open-and-shut and justified case of self-defense, save one wag who pleaded ignorance of the event, declaring, "Am I my brother's keeper?"

To a man, the reporters attested that Tyrone was blameless and that he had demonstrated he was as good a barroom battler as he was a journalist, but that fact didn't keep them from dashing next door to their telegraph keys to flash to their editors the sensational story of an *Evening Telegraph* reporter having drilled to death one of the city's meanest and most despicable characters, all in the defense of a whore.

Later that morning, James Gordon Bennett, Jr. summoned Tyrone downtown to the *Telegram.* "Do you realize the difficulty you've put me in?" the publisher roared as Tyrone stood before him in his opulent Park Row office. "This sordid escapade's going to be in banner headlines in every paper in town with my name next to yours; I am not happy about being associated with a disgusting barroom killing! Do you realize, young man, that since I assumed my father's journalistic mantle and responsibility for two great daily papers, I have been under intense scrutiny? Everyone in New York is waiting for me to fail. Now this! I simply can't continue to employ someone who's shot a man dead in a saloon, however justified you may have been in killing that man, no matter how fine a reporter you may be. Mr. Tyrone, you are dismissed!"

It was, as you will read, the best thing that ever happened to Tyrone.

Part One:

THE BOOK OF FOOLS AND HEROES

PROLOGUE

West from Eden

Two days after being fired by Bennett, delivered to Tyrone's boarding house on Canal Street was the following telegram:

> Superb opportunity awaits you.
> Call upon us at once.
> Beadle and Adams,
> Book Publishers
> 73 William Street.

"Beadle and Adams," he muttered, stuffing the telegram into his pocket. He'd heard of them. They put out a line of popular dime novels. Notorious for their sensationalism, their paperback books covered every lurid aspect known to man. "Superb opportunity awaits you! Now what the hell might that be?"

An hour later, shaved, wearing his best suit and trying not to show his nervousness, he arrived at the Beadle and Adams offices.

"You probably have assumed that we contacted you because of your current notoriety in the daily press regarding the unpleasantness at that drinking establishment," began Adams. A small, balding, pinch-faced man in a plain brown suit, he was dwarfed by a highback leather chair behind an immense desk on one side of a room that seemed to be a mirror-image of the opposite half of the office. "But I assure you, sir, that is not why we have contacted you. No indeed! We have for some time been entertaining the idea of making you a most attractive offer."

As tall and stately as a clipper ship, Adams's partner abruptly rose from behind an identical desk and strode stiffly to a window. In a black suit, he was silhouetted against a glass that afforded a view of a forest of masts of an armada of merchant vessels docked along the cluttered North River waterfront. "Are you a traveling man, Mr. Tyrone?" he asked, turning slowly. "Ever been out west?"

"Our readers are fascinated by the far frontier, Mr. Tyrone," interjected Adams enthusiastically. "They're hungry for stories of the wild and woolly! Can't get enough of them."

"Farthest west I've been is Hoboken," said Tyrone.

"The description of you in the day's press is that of a capable, tough and resourceful young man," said Beadle in a tone as stiff as his collar. "I believe I can quote one of the newspapers exactly: 'Tyrone is a rough and tough fellow but has a keen sense of righteousness, justice and an ample amount of chivalry.' "

"That's pretty generous," said Tyrone, embarrassed.

"We know from having followed your work for some time in the *Evening Telegraph* that your writing skills are unsurpassed," continued Beadle. "Until now we entertained no hope of benefiting from your talents. But, unfortunately for you and perhaps fortunately for us, you suddenly find yourself without employment. I expect you are quite likely to remain so until this current scandal is forgotten. Wouldn't you agree?"

"Looks that way."

"That is why Mr. Beadle and I have invited you here at this time," said Adams. He leaned forward from the depths of his immense canyon-like chair. "We have a proposition for you."

Tyrone threw open his arms. "I'm all ears!"

Beadle returned to his desk, sitting behind it with the sharp point of his chin resting on the steeple of slender hands pressed together as if in prayer. "We are interested in engaging you to go out to the frontier and dig up some stories for our readers."

"What kind of stories?"

"The romance of the West!" chirped Adams.

"Is it romantic?"

"The place is teeming with colorful characters," answered Beadle.

"Outlaws," exclaimed Adams.

"What makes outlaws romantic?"

"The imagination of people," said Beadle. "If the people get it into their minds that the outlaws of the wild and woolly West are romantic, that makes them so. We are in the business of catering to the romantic imaginations of our readers."

"The pay is good and there's a generous expense allowance," declared Adams, his eyes twinkling impishly.

"What about royalties?"

"Five percent of the selling price," said Adams.

Impatiently, Beadle drummed long fingers atop his desk. "If you wish to mull this over, we'll understand."

Tyrone shrugged. "Make it ten percent and there's nothing to mull. There's really nothing to keep me in New York."

Smiling slyly, Adams, opened his desk drawer. "We have a contract ready."

With an admiring laugh, Tyrone noted the royalty already written in: ten percent.

From his desk, Beadle flourished a thatch of railway tickets. "These will take you as far as Kansas City. So long as you send us thrillingly romantic stories of the Wild West, Mr. Tyrone, where you go from there is entirely up to you."

ONE

West-bound Train

Studying a gold pocket watch cradled in his cupped hand, the short young man standing in blistering sun just below Tyrone's window should have been overheated in his blue conductor's tunic dotted by a double row of brass buttons, sharply creased matching pants and a jaunty pill-box hat with a patent leather bill, but Tyrone thought he looked as cool as a cucumber. Pocketing the timepiece, he peered forward to the engine, wagged his arms and bellowed, "All ah-BAWD!"

A second later, with a belch of gritty gray smoke from a diamond stack, four blasts of steam that swirled around the wheels like fog and a warning shriek of its whistle, the black locomotive nosed ahead. It set off a jerking, clanging and rattling of couplers and a sneeze-like shudder that wrenched through a wood-piled tender, a slat-sided livestock car loaded with nervous horses, two boxcars, a dust-coated red baggage car and a yellow-sided passenger coach with grime-streaked windows.

One hour late, this was the 1:50 P.M. departing west-bound out of Topeka, the capital city of Kansas.

Seated at the rear of the crowded coach, Tyrone was

glad to be on his way at last and gladder to have the car's only empty seat beside him, highly suitable for stretching out. Slumping, he shut his eyes, but immediately across his face fell an ominous shadow—a cloud blotting the sun, he supposed, until out of it, as deep and rumbling as thunder, boomed a voice. " 'Scuse me!"

Through the slits of half-opened eyes, Tyrone peered up at a fat man looming in the aisle. An overweening giant with a handlebar mustache and dressed in a coal-black suit, white shirt and red bowtie, he asked, "Anybody sittin' there?"

Tyrone lurched upright. "No. Help yourself."

"Much obliged," said the fat man, slinging a carpetbag onto the overhead baggage rack. "Nearly missed the train! Ran like the devil and leaped for dear life to catch it. This was the only unoccupied seat I could find and I was afraid you was savin' it for somebody and I'd have to stand till we get to the next stop." He thudded into the vacancy and wiped his damp face with a handkerchief that looked as big as a tablecloth and as red as his florid, moon face. "Not even hell can be as hot as Kansas in summer. How far you headin', mister?"

"Wichita."

"Ah, the new boom town of the cattle trade, down on the Arkansas River. Headin' there myself."

Politeness more than an interest in his new companion prompted Tyrone's reply. "You're in the cattle business?"

"Shoot no. I got more sense than that," said the fat man, shifting to remove his coat, undo his tie and stuff his shirttail into his pants. "I'm a drummer peddlin' a line of tools and hardware for a big outfit in Kansas City. My samples are up ahead in the baggage car. There's a thrivin' market for construction implements, don't you know; what with all the buildin' goin' on in Wichita. Yessiree, the place is on a kick, though there's no tellin' how long it's gonna last. Could be that it'll be a flash in the pan, maybe a one- or two-year sensation like Abilene and

Newton were. It all depends on where the railroad goes next and how soon. It's the Texas cattle trade that determines whether a place survives, you see. If the cattlemen fancy a spot, then it benefits from trail-worn, sensation-starved cowboys throwin' around their wages. Where there's beef on the hoof, there's money to be made. Have you ever been to a cow town?"

"Nope. Wouldn't know a cowboy from a fence post."

"Didn't think so. Your suit of clothes is obviously from way back East. And it's plain you haven't been out in the sun much."

"You're very observant."

"A salesman's gotta be, don't you know?"

"You're familiar with cow towns on account of your trade?"

"You hit the nail on the head, friend. M'name's Hicks, by the way; Henry Hicks, known to my customers and friends as Big Hank." He patted his large belly. "You can see why."

"I'm Harry Tyrone."

"Pleased to make your acquaintance," said Hicks, offering a damp hand that for one who handled building supplies was as soft as a down pillow.

"I've heard that a cow town can be pretty wild and woolly," said Tyrone. Indeed, the hope of running into some compelling tales of the cow towns had put him on this train, he reminded himself. "Lots of excitement? Plenty of cowboys? Gunplay?"

"What goes on in those places will open your eyes, Harry. May I call you Harry? Take it from me, when those cowhands cut loose after sundown, a cow town resembles a hell even the devil would find testy. Brass bands whooping it up, hack drivers yelling and cursing, saloons operatin' at full tilt, card sharps and, of course, plenty of loose women. I reckon a cow town is the most wanton and abandoned place on earth."

Worse than New York's Tenderloin district? Tyrone wondered, doubtfully.

"It's strictly business that takes me out to Wichita," continued Hicks. "I would not live there if you paid me to."

"I'm not planning on staying." Long enough to find a good story and move on to the next one; that's my plan, Tyrone thought. "Have they got a decent hotel?"

"A few, plus some boarding houses. The best hotels are the Harris, the Occidental and the Douglas Avenue House, where I usually put up. Of course, after ridin' on this Atchison, Topeka and Santa Fe rattler, anything'll look good in the way of comfort. How far have you come, by the way? Where'd you hail from?"

"New York City."

Hicks bolted upright with a look of amazement. He scratched his mustache. "Whoo-ee, you left the comforts and delights of the big city for god-forsaken Wichita? Lord, what in blazes for?"

Peering through the window at the last outskirts of Topeka sliding away and a stretch of sunlit summer-green prairie grass coming into view, Tyrone considered replying, "Fate brought me here. You see, there was this whore in a saloon and . . ." But with a whisper of a smile, he answered, "It's a long story."

"Most are," sighed Hicks, knowing from experience when to let a subject drop.

Half an hour out of Topeka, Tyrone saw his first Indian. A nearly naked youth as slender as a reed with burnished skin and long black hair streaming behind him like a flag, he raced the train astride a horse the color of red clay.

"Don't worry. He's a harmless redskin," said Hicks. "One of the Kansa tribe, also known as the Kaw. They're very peaceable. Your scalp is quite safe, Harry. This is their territory we're passin' through; the valley of the Neosha."

The Indian lost the race, dwindling to a speck in the distance as the train ascended from the pretty valley onto grassy flatlands that Tyrone found to be a marvel of openness. On the trains that had transported him in reasonable comfort from New York, he'd looked out of windows at a vast but settled land where only a few miles had separated the teeming cities of the Atlantic coast and the quiet towns, villages and hamlets inland. There'd been wider stretches of land between the houses in the patchwork quilt of farms in the rich country flanking the railways that had carried him to the sprawl of Chicago and then into the bustle of Kansas City, but nothing had prepared him for this seemingly endless Kansas prairie that looked like a limitless, empty sea of grass. "Wide-open territory, isn't it?"

The fat man at his side turned a listless, droopy eyed sidelong look. "Beg pardon?"

Tyrone kept his eyes toward the land. "I had no idea how big and empty it would be out here."

"Don't worry. It'll be crowded enough where you're goin', even for a city boy."

Presently, the train reached the town of Burlingame, which through Tyrone's window didn't appear to be worth the waste of a ten-minute stop. Four passengers got off—a man and woman and their two children.

Forty miles farther, Emporia was next, little better than Burlingame, Tyrone concluded, but providing a half-hour pause. "Now's the time to stretch your legs and relieve your kidneys," advised Tyrone's companion, lumbering into the aisle. "That's a travelin' man's first rule of survival when arrivin' in a new place," he continued. "Before you enter, take a moment to piss and count your money. The salesman's other rules for gettin' along are: never draw to an inside straight, never trust a walleyed horse and don't take the word of a woman with black underwear."

When the train departed Emporia, the passenger coach

was full again, heading almost due west, but soon it swung southwesterly with the sun ahead and slightly to the right so that Tyrone could see the shadow of the entire train racing alongside the track as the laboring locomotive spewed a long tail of gray smoke that smudged the cloudless sky for miles behind.

Newton was next. "This was last year's flash in the pan. I made quite a lot of money here," said the salesman. "It's a dying town now, if it ain't dead already."

Tyrone gazed down the platform where only the conductor stood in his blue outfit, studying his gold watch, then past him and the ramshackle depot to a tangle of wooden fences that were the corrals which a year ago had been thronged with longhorn Texas cattle that this year were going elsewhere.

At the last minute, two young men leapt aboard. Rawboned and lanky with faces that were suntanned and leathery, they had to stand, leaning against the door in weather-bleached blue workshirts with red scarves around their necks and scruffy-looking jeans stuffed into the tops of knee-high buckskin boots. Long brown hair flowed out from under high, broad-brimmed hats stained by sweat. Wide black belts studded with cartridge loops slanted across their flat bellies, tugged downward by the weight of sixguns in holsters that were cinched to their thighs with rawhide thongs.

"There's a couple of hardcases," whispered Hicks.

"You know 'em?" Tyrone replied.

"The Ludlum boys," said Hicks, wrinkling his nose. "Mickey and Moe. They think they're something but they're too dumb to see that what they are is fools. They're cousins, and as brassy a pair of owlhoots as ever saddled up."

"A pair of owl . . . whats?"

"Owlhoots. Troublemakers. Good-for-nuthin's. They're a couple of no-accounts and drifters who've stirred up trouble everywhere they set foot, but they're tinhorn gunslicks who think they're the James Boys. You've heard about them?"

"A bit."

"Now there's a pair of bandits you gotta admire! They're Missouri boys but they seem to range far and wide. I happened to be in the town of Corydon over in Iowa two years ago when they stuck up a bank and got away with fifty thousand dollars." He paused with admiration lighting up his eyes. "Whee-oo, what I could do with that kind of money," he continued. "But I'm afraid I don't have the grit it takes to march into a bank and liberate its holdings, much as I might like to."

"Wichita is next," shouted the conductor, striding the length of the coach. "Next and last stop is Wichita."

As he passed, Tyrone asked, "How long till we arrive?"

The conductor fished out his gold watch. "About an hour."

"Is there a telegraph office?"

"They got everything in Wichita," said the conductor, pocketing the watch.

A telegram to Beadle and Adams informing them of his arrival at Wichita would be in order, decided Tyrone as the train swung due south. Soon, the featureless prairie gave way to gently rolling landscape and by dusk the train was dipping into a shallow valley and running beside a muddy river flanked by stands of cooling cottonwoods. Then, suddenly, they were crossing a vast clearing—a stretch of openness that looked to Tyrone as if a giant had gone through with a scythe, leveling everything to make way for a cluster of buildings and sheds that looked raw and unvarnished.

The conductor bellowed, "Everybody gets off at Wichita."

Dripping sweat from his jowls, Hicks lumbered down from the coach. "I wish you luck in your endeavors," he said, waving as he proceeded toward the baggage car to retrieve his samples.

The Ludlums were last off, swaggering away with their bootheels banging the planks and six-shooters swaying at their sides.

"Owlhoots," muttered Tyrone, liking the sound of the word.

Inside the new train depot, he dictated as a telegrapher tapped his message to Beadle and Adams directly out on his key:

ARRIVED OUT WEST
ALL GOING WELL
START EXPLORING
ON OWLHOOT TRAIL
TOMORROW REGARDS
TYRONE

TWO

The Wichita Story

Only God knows how many years had passed prior to Tyrone's arrival in Wichita since the first traveler had paused in the shade of ash, elm, hackberry, burr oak and tall cottonwoods to rest and drink from the clear, cool water of the joining of two rivers that someone would eventually name the Arkansas and the Little Arkansas. It had been an Indian, of course, probably an Osage.

The first of the men like Tyrone didn't come until just before the Civil War but they were restless and roaming white men—wanderers, trappers and buffalo hunters who left footprints, not settlements.

Then came the Wichitas. A peaceable tribe from farther south who built grass huts in the shape of bee hives, they had been forced to become refugees by the war and longed to go back to their roots. Accompanying them to their new land was a resourceful trader, Jesse Chisholm, who hauled merchandise from San Antonio deep in the heart of Texas to his post that thrived among the Wichitas. The tribe packed up soon after the war and returned to their native homeland, leaving the territory around the two

Arkansas rivers up for grabs at precisely the time when cattlemen in Texas were desperately seeking markets.

Encouraged by a handful of enterprising livestock dealers who were anticipating the inevitable westward expansion of the railroads through Kansas, the Texans started their herds of sturdy longhorns up Chisholm's trail. The first of them arrived at the stockyards of the Kansas Pacific Railway at Abilene in the summer of 1867.

In April of the following year, as President Andrew Johnson was appointing a commission to negotiate a land treaty with the Osage Indians that would encompass the land surrounding the two Arkansas rivers, a group of speculators, noting the success of Abilene, gathered at Emporia to form the Wichita Town and Land Company. Their purpose was the creation of a metropolis that would become the center of the cattle trade astride the Atchison, Topeka and Santa Fe line.

That same year, E.S. Munger built the Munger House hotel and an enterprising settler built the "first and last chance saloon" where cattlemen could purchase their first drink since coming up Jesse Chisholm's trail from Texas and their last before heading back down.

By August 1869, Wichita was already a town of two or three hundred inhabitants. A year later it boasted 175 buildings, including three churches, a masonic hall, three hotels, stores of every kind, two stage lines, enough residents to vote the town the seat of government of Sedgwick County and a handful of places where a man could get a drink.

At long last, in May 1872, the AT&SF's railway tracks were in place and soon the first train rumbled into the brand-new depot for a wildly jubilant celebration of Wichita's debut as the first town north of the Red River to be served by a railroad.

Eleven months later, when Tyrone stepped onto the plank platform of the station on a sultry evening in June, the arrival of a train had become commonplace in a spot where a traveler who sought to rest and refresh himself did not have to hunker down under the trees like the unknown Indian of Wichita's beginnings.

To slake a thirst in June '73, a man had his choice of first class saloons such as the Syndicate, Spirit Bank, Gold Room and Long Charlie Carew's fancy resort recently transplanted from Abilene.

To lay down his head Tyrone had his choice of eight hotels.

He elected the Harris House because it was closest to the depot. Too travel-weary to have a meal, he went directly to bed and slept like a baby. Hugged by the feathery mattress of a vast brass bed, he slept until mid-afternoon.

Naked, he sat on the edge of the bed listening to the sounds of commerce clattering up from the street and drifting through the open window of his front room on the second floor.

Scrubbing off the grime of travel with a yellow bar of medicinal-smelling soap and tepid water poured from a porcelain pitcher into a china bowl, he assayed himself as reflected in a free-standing, full-length, oval-shaped, gilt-edged mirror, the likes of which he hadn't seen since his last visit to Mary Divine's whorehouse at the corner of West Street and Christopher on the North River water-front the night before he'd headed west. The salesman on the train had been right about him in every aspect, he decided as he dried himself with a coarse towel. "East-erner" was written all over him.

Shaving, he studied his pale face and remembered the leathery flesh of the Ludlum boys in their worn and weathered clothes and scuffed boots with inch-thick heels. Rising on his toes, he projected with some pleasure that boots like theirs would add a welcome inch to the five-feet-six that he'd been stuck at since the age of fifteen.

The rest of what he saw in the individual he found re-flected in the gaudy-fringed glass was far more satisfactory than his abbreviated height—a thick mane of wavy brown hair with a reddish tinge that the girl at Mary Divine's had judged to be as fine as cornsilk. He saw a boyish face women had always fancied, eyes that Ben Turner had described as "observant as a hawk's" and which his mother once said were as green and honest as the grass of Ireland, and a trim build which Seamus McGlory had discerned to be worthy of the prize-fight ring.

Flattered by the notion, he'd considered boxing until Ben Turner heaped the idea with threatening scorn. "That's about the dumbest thing you could do with your life," he'd grumbled over a mug of beer at McGlory's. "You've got brains, kid, and I'll be damned if I'll stand still for you getting them beaten out."

"Good old Ben," Tyrone whispered as he crouched into a boxer's stance. Balling his fists, he shot the left toward the figure in the mirror. Tapping the reflected chin with a right, he grunted, "Knockout!"

At that moment, the ebb and flow of the hubbub outside reaching a new peak attracted his attention. Leaning out the window, he peered down at a wide, muddy, stinking and shadeless street baking in a shimmering glare. Into the din, he yelled "Hello, Wichita" but none of the swarming, sweating people below appeared to hear him.

In the shade of the porch of the hotel, he paused to watch a passing parade of people. He was made painfully aware of being a stranger, sticking out like a sore thumb with his pale face and New York tailoring while those he viewed were as brown as berries as they milled and sauntered and hurried and thronged Main and Douglas Streets. There was a variety of costumes: checkered outfits worn by eastern sharps, gamblers and confidence men; sleek and well dressed speculators with airs of genteel living and stuffed purses; rough-threaded independent cattle drovers looking for buyers and top prices; reckless, footloose and carefree paid-off sunburned cowboys straight off the trail in worn jeans, chaps and weathered hats; a pair of brown-skinned men with floppy sombreros, legs wrapped in flapping leather chaps and shoulders draped by serapes; the buckskin breeches and jackets of a pair of grizzled plainsmen; friendly Indians in brightly colored blanket togas leading paint ponies; and the somber preacher-like suits of business-minded men prepared to buy Texas beef on the hoof.

Joining the parade to explore the town, he counted two hardware stores, a druggist's, a pair of bootmakers, a saddlery and harness store, four real estate offices, a jewelry shop and two banks before he was stopped dead in his tracks in front of a formidable brick structure.

Painted in white in a window was a sign:

THE WICHITA EAGLE
Marshall M. Murdock
Editor

"I'll be damned," he said aloud. "They've got themselves a newspaper in this burg!"

Opening a plain varnished door, he stepped from the hot brightness of the street into the dim cool of an office redolent with the pleasant, dank, familiar and welcoming odor of printer's ink and the crisp, clean aroma of fresh newsprint.

Beyond the hulk of a printing press at a desk bathed in the light of an oil lamp in a corner of the cluttered room, a man with a bushy mustache and long sideburns looked up curiously from beneath an editor's green eyeshade. "Can I help you?"

Tyrone blurted, "I'm a newspaperman myself."

"Sorry, mister," barked the man at the desk. "I've got no jobs available."

"Oh, I'm not looking for work," exclaimed Tyrone, striding toward the desk. "Tyrone's my name, late of the New York *Evening Telegram.*"

Tapping a pencil on the desk, the man at the desk rared back. "That's Mr. James Gordon Bennett's newspaper!"

Tyrone grinned proudly. "That's right. But I gave up working for it to come out here on behalf of the publishing firm of Beadle and Adams to write a book about cowboys."

"That's a switch. It's been my experience that all the writing about cowboys is done entirely by people back East who'd die if they stepped in cow shit; more fiction than fact."

"My book will be the truth, sir, I assure you!"

"I'm Murdock, editor of this little sheet. My friends call me Marsh. My enemies have more picturesque nicknames for me." Standing, he rose taller than Tyrone expected. His handshake was iron. "How can I be of help to you?"

"Well, I guess I could use a shove in the right direction."

Murdock chuckled. "Sounds more like a job for a preacher than a newspaper editor. What is it you want to be shoved at?"

"Toward a genuine example of a Texas cowboy, I suppose."

"You'll find that breed congregated mostly across the river in a section of town called Delano. That's the district where most of the hell-raising takes place. If you can wait a couple of minutes I'll be happy to escort you. Do you have a horse?"

Tyrone shrugged. "Afraid not."

"Doesn't matter. I've got a buggy. But if you've come all the way from New York to write the truth about cowboys you'll be needing a horse. Best place to buy one is over at Arnold's Stable. You *can* ride?"

"Haven't been thrown by a nag yet!"

Murdock laughed, a thunderclap in the tight confines of the room. "Have a seat. I'll only be a few minutes."

When they stepped outside, the sun was going down and a breeze was up, taking the hard edge off the heat. "The corner of Main and Douglas may not be as busy as the intersection of Broadway and Fifth Avenue," said Murdock, "but it'll do."

THREE

Murdock's Story

"It's amazing to see how much this place has grown up just in the little over a year that I've been here," said Murdock. As if for punctuation, he flicked a buggy whip to the rump of a handsome chestnut buggy horse. "It's all due to the coming of the railroad, of course. No trains, no cattle trade; simple as that," he said, needling the trim black rig through the clog of horses, wagons and people that constituted the traffic mayhem that was the main intersection of Wichita.

Tyrone asked, "Where were you before you landed here?"

"You're a newspaperman, all right," said Murdock with a chuckle and a quick sidelong look. Stroking the brown sideburns that flowed down from his jaw like a pair of brooms, he answered, "I came here from Burlingame. That's the 'where' of it. Shall I give you the rest of the journalist's list of queries, those trusty five W's? Who, what, where, when and why?"

"I gave you mine. Seems only fair I get your full bill of particulars."

"Shall I start with my age? You should always put the person's age in your story, right?"

"You're around thirty, I'd guess."

"Close enough."

"Born back East?"

"How do you figure that?"

"Wasn't everybody in the West born back East?"

"Pretty near, I expect," said Murdock, guiding them into the middle of the street.

"College man?" asked Tyrone.

"I was going to attend but didn't."

"How come?"

"Getting on with life seemed more important. Then along came the War, which was an educational experience."

"Union or Confederate?"

"I donned the blue. After that I came out to Kansas. It was a good decision. There turned out to be an opportunity to edit the local paper in Burlingame. Soon, politics interested me. I served two years in the Kansas legislature, learning things they also don't teach in college. I'm a Republican, by the way. You strike me as a Democrat."

"As a matter of fact, I am, but I hope you won't hold it against me. Besides, it's you we're talking about."

"When Wichita was being organized, some of the notables invited me to set up a newspaper here that would express a Republican viewpoint. I bought equipment and supplies in St. Louis. The first *Eagle* appeared in April last year."

"That must have been quite a thrill, having a newspaper to call your own."

"I'll say," grunted Murdock. "Then came the railroad to Wichita," he continued, carried forward by the rush of memories. "The first train pulled into town on May 11, 1872 freighted with the great expectations of the people of Wichita. Everything was pinned on the arrival of Texas cattle. Would they come? Might they go somewhere else?

The town of Ellsworth was trying very hard to persuade the cattlemen to go there. But that October I climbed to the roof of the tallest building in town, looked out over the range to the south and east, and counted twenty-one herds grazing within two miles of the town. That was also quite a thrill!"

They'd come to a bridge and a large sign:

LEAVE YOUR REVOLVERS
AT POLICE HEADQUARTERS
AND GET A CHECK.
Marshal Michael Meagher

"I'm sad to say that Mike's sign is honored more in the breech than the observance," said Murdock, shaking his head ruefully. "The marshal does the best he can but the numbers are against him. With hundreds of cowhands pouring in from the trail, he just can't keep up. Do you carry a weapon, Mr. Tyrone?"

"Should I?"

"Only if you can handle one."

A picture of Crazy Sid lying dead in the Garden of Eden stabbed into Tyrone's mind. "I assure you, sir, if I did get a gun it would be strictly for self-defense."

"Good man," said Murdock, flicking the chestnut's rump with the reins. "Didn't mean to lecture," he went on as the buggy rattled onto the bridge. "I try to limit my pontificating to my editorials in the *Eagle.* Don't jump to the conclusion that Wichitans are a bunch of stick-in-the-muds. They just want law and order, with their consequent peace and security. You see, it will be bad for Wichita if the persons who frequent the city show a reckless disregard for law and order. Should that element get the upper hand, then we may be certain that business men, men with capital and men having families will steer clear of Wichita. Nothing would more surely kill the rapid and substantial growth of our city."

Tyrone threw up his hands. "I promise to behave myself!"

"Please don't get the idea that Wichitans are against folks having a good time. Hell, the first thing the county commissioners did at their first meeting back in '70 was issue a saloon license!"

The buggy bumped its way off the bridge.

Before them stretched a wide dirt thoroughfare that had been stomped flat by the hooves of horses and cattle and men in high-heeled boots and baked hard by the unrelenting sun of the hot, rainless summer. As best Tyrone could see, its entire length was flanked by two uneven rows of low buildings whose painted fronts were festooned with the enticing signs, of saloons, dance halls, keno rooms and poker parlors. Large windows spilled inviting light across the plank sidewalks and into the street that was as crowded and animated as the Bowery or Broadway's raucous Tenderloin on any night in his experience.

"Welcome to Delano," announced Murdock, drawing rein. "Best thing to do is park the buggy and hoof it."

"It's damned friendly and accommodating of you to show me around, Mr. Murdock."

"Not at all," said the newspaperman as he climbed down from the rig. Looping the horse's reins around a hitching rail, he said, "I'm sure you'd do the same for me if I ever got to New York. Visiting fireman! And please call me Marsh."

"I'm used to answering to Tyrone. Seems to be a tradition amongst the ink-stained wretches of Park Row—last names; don't know why."

"There's a lot about the newspaper trade that doesn't make sense," chuckled Murdock as Tyrone hopped down. "The whole enterprise is built on bad news. That stems from human nature, doesn't it? It seems that nothing attracts one man's attention like another man's business, especially if it's trouble. It's the bad news that makes the biggest headlines. Can you name me a town or city any place that doesn't have more saloons than churches?"

"Not readily," chuckled Tyrone.

"Yeah, the human race has a strong attachment to the bad. Been so since Adam and Eve. I wish things were different out here, but they aren't. Towns like this one draw a bad element. It's the idea of easy money that brings them, of course. Like the man said, 'The love of money is the root of all evil.' You'll see some of that this evening here in Delano and, who knows, maybe you'll run into the very story you came all this way looking for! The best place to start, I think, is at Long Charlie's."

FOUR

Long Charlie's

Before Wichita, Long Charlie Carew had been in the business of selling liquor to cowboys in Abilene where his first emporium was one of the first of the many saloons that were to sprout like mushrooms on Texas Street, catering to the thirsts of cowboys straight off the Chisholm Trail with their wages burning holes in their pockets. It had been a well-lighted room on the ground floor entered through emerald-green batwing doors. The bar was mahogany with a brass rail. Behind it on a shelf stood a forest of whiskey bottles made to look even more numerous by mirrors interrupted at intervals of five feet by gilt-framed paintings of voluptuous naked women especially chosen during a week he'd spent in St. Louis purchasing the furnishings. To the left for those who wanted to sit down to drink were tables and chairs. At the back, larger tables were arranged for the customers who might fancy poker, faro or monte. Soon there would be a roulette table.

For those with a yen for women, Charlie enlisted seven professionals from Kansas City brothels on terms that allowed them to keep all their earnings, the saloon's profit flowing from a small fee payable at the bar in advance of going upstairs to three bedrooms on a nightly-rental basis or to a half-dozen curtained cubicles that could be engaged by the half-hour containing a bed, a chair, a lamp, a stand with a porcelain water pitcher, wash bowl and towels and a line of nails in the wall to hang clothing and six-guns.

Being Irish and gifted with gab, Charlie was a natural as a host and a bartender and it was his Gaelic charm as much as the whiskey, the gambling and the women that instantly turned the place into a roaring success.

Those attributes also proved reliable when he transported his salooning enterprise lock, stock and barrel to the town of Newton following the collapse of the Abilene cattle market and, when Newton folded, to Wichita, taking up space in Delano and competing robustly with Rowdy Joe's, the Alamo Beer Garden, Syndicate, Spirit Bank and Gold Room.

In all of these incarnations, Long Charlie's was hallmarked by the emerald-green batwings, recognized by veterans of the cattle drives as the sign of a place where a cowboy always got a square deal for his money.

When Marsh Murdock shoved them open and Tyrone stepped into the saloon, Tyrone thought he'd been catapulted back to McGlory's Garden of Eden as he faced the huge, brightly lit room and was swamped by the roar of baritone voices and the smells of beer, tobacco smoke and sweat, although the bar was not McGlory's O but a straight line down the right side. Behind it, four capable-looking men in white aprons plucked bottles from stocks that filled a stretch of double shelves interrupted only by a pair of gaudy gilt-framed mirrors and an oval-shaped painting of a reclining naked woman. Shoulder-to-shoulder facing these enticements were thirsty young men in weathered hats, work shirts, bandanas, boots and jeans with wages burning holes in the pockets. Lording it over them and the bartenders as he paced behind the bar was one of the tallest men Tyrone had ever seen; an elongated McGlory, at least seven feet high.

"Charlie, c'mere!" shouted Murdock, wiggling a finger at him.

"If you've come round to try to sell me an advert for that rag of yours," bellowed the tall man, loping forward behind the bar, "forgit it!"

"I want you to meet Tyrone," said Murdock. "Fresh from back East."

"I'd a never guessed it," said the tall man, squinting as he surveyed Tyrone from head to foot. "I seen my share of greenhorns but this fella's downright emerald in hue."

"That's because my folks came from Ireland," retorted Tyrone.

"With that baby face of yours, as Irish as Paddy's pig, who'd a not guessed it? And you're about as tall as a leprechaun to boot."

"Meet Charlie Carew, famous all over the frontier for his tact," said Murdock.

"No offense intended," said Carew.

"None taken," said Tyrone, turning to survey the room. Fiercely attentive to a game of five card stud, he noted, were a pair of dusty cowboys and the Ludlum cousins.

At the rear of the room another pair of cowboys tossed darts with obvious ignorance of the rules of the game. "I see you've got a dart board."

"Ah, you're a dart thrower, are ye?" asked Carew.

"Used to be back home."

"Tyrone's come here from New York to collect material for a book he's writing," said Murdock.

Carew pitched forward, leaning across the bar supported by the stilts of his arms. "Honestly, I can think of no one more suitable to be written up in a book than yours truly," he said excitedly. "My life is a fascinatin' tale."

"The man's interested in cowboys," said Murdock.

Carew jerked up straight. "Gawd, whatever for? You

can tell a cowboy's story in eight little words. 'A fool and his money is soon parted!' "

"And none quicker than the one who stumbles into Long Charlie's," laughed Murdock, turning to survey the crowded room. "You name it and Long Charlie's place has got it."

"What's your poison, Tyrone?" asked Carew. "The first drink is on the house."

"Seeing as how I'm a leprechaun, have you got any Irish whiskey?"

"Is the Pope Italian? And what about you, Marsh? Your usual?"

"Of course. And bring it to my usual table, please," said the editor.

"Mr. Murdock always takes a seat in the rear of the place back to the wall, facing the door," Carew explained to Tyrone as he turned to gather a bottle of Irish whiskey and Murdock's bourbon. "He figures that way he'll never get shot in the back."

On the way to a table in the corner only big enough for two, Tyrone glanced down at the poker game featuring the Ludlums. Catching the eye of one of them, he said, "Howdy," smiling, but went unanswered.

Murdock looked quizzical. "Do you know Mickey Ludlum?"

"Nah. He came in on the same train as me."

"If you want a villain for your book, you won't find a worse one than Mickey Ludlum, believe me. His cousin Moe's a close second."

"A man next to me on the train half-expected them to rob it," chuckled Tyrone.

"It's a wonder they didn't," replied Murdock, pulling out a chair with its back to the wall.

"Who'd want to shoot you, Marsh?" asked Tyrone.

"A Democrat, most likely," jibed Carew as he set down their bottles and glasses.

"I choose this spot not out of concern for my safety,"

said Murdock as Carew departed, towering over everyone as he made his way to the bar. "I sit here because I can observe the entire place. I'm a born people watcher. Folks fascinate me. I suppose that's why the newspaper business got its hooks into me. And politics. Maybe that's part of why I decided to come out West after the war. I was interested in the idea of so many people starting over, getting a fresh start for themselves. That's the story you should put into any books you write. But I'm a realist. I know that what the readers of Beadle and Adams books want is not the story of people building a country but the sensational, romantic aspects. The cowboys!"

"Aren't cowboys people? I'd wager that each of these fellows lined up at Charlie's bar has a story to tell. In his own way, each one is a hero. Every man is the hero of his own life story."

"You're a romantic, all right," scoffed Murdock, pouring his bourbon.

Tyrone shrugged and gazed down at the shot glass clutched in the curl of his hand. "Is that bad?"

"Hell no. It's totally understandable that you've come here thinking that every night in a cow town is nothing but guns going off and dead bodies littering the floor. Lord knows there's been some of that, although not as much as a lot of people have come to believe. But cheer up. If you hang around the human race long enough, something'll pop." He peered through the smoke haze at the Ludlums. "Maybe Mickey and Moe will rip the joint up!"

With a half-smile, Tyrone asked, "Which is which?"

"The taller one with the scar on his cheek is Mickey. He's also the oldest. Claims he got the scar in a knife fight with a Cherokee down in the Indian Territory. The truth is he was slashed by a whore he tried to beat up in a house up in Abilene."

"Sweet," grunted Tyrone.

"But it's the little one, Moe, who's the really dangerous one because he goes crazy at the drop of a hat. The story he'd have you believe is that a horse kicked him in the head when he was a kid. But it was his father who whacked him with a shovel."

"They look peaceful enough tonight."

"They're fine if nothing riles them."

"Then I'll try not to rile them."

FIVE

The Herd

More than a year before Tyrone headed west, at a spot twenty miles south of the meeting of the Arkansas and the Little Arkansas, Charlie Carew had planted a sign:

EVERYTHING GOES
IN WICHITA
BE SURE TO VISIT
LONG CHARLIE'S SALOON

The only object rising above the foot-high grass of the featureless plain between it and the northern horizon, it was ten feet wide and six high with bright red letters against canary yellow and had been canted slightly backward by a cyclone that autumn.

Gaping at it in wonder on this blistering July afternoon, the caporal of the Colter herd declared, "First I ever seen anythin' like it." A small man with bronze skin, and a drooping brown mustache, the Mexican tilted back his sombrero. Wiping the sweat from his wide brow with a blue bandana, he looked sidelong at his trail boss squinting in the glare. "What do you figure it means?"

With a shake of his head and two strokes of his thumb to a wispy blond mustache that he'd been trying and failing to grow to the satisfactory dimensions of the Mexican's since he was a cavalryman in the War, Morgan said, "Just what it says, I reckon. I happen to know the fella who put up that advertisement. And if Charlie Carew says they got everything in Wichita and in Wichita everything goes, it must be a hell of a wide open town. I just hope that it's also got a bunch of buyers willing to pay decent prices for cattle."

"They'll pay," asserted the caporal confidently, cocking his head to their rear, " 'cause it's the best herd we've had."

"Yeah, Dalgo, they're mighty fine," said Morgan, peering back admiringly. "They've covered the drive very well."

He lifted his weathered old cavalry hat and ran his fingers through a mane of damped-down and sweat-matted yellow hair and then swabbed his lean, angular, sun-leathered face with a blue and white wipe. Replacing the hat, he jammed all but a small corner of the kerchief into the back pocket of his trail-broken Levi Strauss jeans and stood in the stirrups. Picking at his faded blue cotton workshirt and the seat of his pants, he unglued them from his sweat-slicked chest, back and rump. Easing down into the saddle, he muttered, "Cussed heat!"

Early the next morning, leaving the caporal in charge of the herd on a sprawling grazing camp south and west of the Arkansas, he rode into Wichita.

There, perched on the top of a rail fence affording a view of bewildered cattle being prodded up a loading chute and into a gently rocking slat-sided box car, the sixth in a string of three already filled and four waiting to be, Joseph G. McCoy was attired for business, as usual, in a black suit, white shirt, black necktie and derby that always made Morgan think of him as a preacher rather than the savvy businessman. He almost single-handedly had wedded Kansas to Texas by creating markets along the westward-progressing railroads and then persuading cattlemen to drive their herds a thousand miles north along the Chisholm Trail to meet the trains. He shifted his eyes only momentarily from the loading chute as Morgan rode up. "Welcome to Wichita," he said. "I figured you'd show up sooner or later."

Stepping from his horse directly to the fence, Morgan said, "The place seems to be thriving."

"Boom now, bust tomorrow. That's the cattle business," said McCoy knowingly as Morgan settled beside him.

"How's prices?"

"It's a seller's market at the moment. Your timing's right."

"Glad to hear it. I got eight thousand head of the best beeves."

"I've got you a buyer representing a Chicago syndicate who'll take about a thousand."

"That's good for starters."

"They're putting up over at the Munger House. Meet me there at noon. We'll have a meal, close the deal and catch up on old times. How's that sound?"

"Appetizin'," grinned Morgan.

When the rumbling started the next morning, Tyrone was asleep, but as the steady, low drumbeat of thousands of hooves belonging to Morgan's cattle grew, the whole hotel trembled and his big brass bed danced a jig and started inching across the floor, shaking him awake. Bolting upright, he bellowed, "Jesus Christ Almighty."

A mist of dust drifted down from the slats of the ceiling and settled like snow on his tangled hair and bare shoulders. The overhead lamp swayed and the wash bowl and water pitcher rattled on the sideboard.

Expecting a collapse and grabbing for his pants, he heard a sound that seemed like the cries of a million souls burning in the bowels of Hell, as if he'd died in his sleep and plunged, room and all, into that hideous place of fire and brimstone he'd been warned about so often by the

Bible-thumping preachers who blossomed on street corners every Saturday night on the Bowery.

Gulping breath, he became aware of a strange, smell—an overpowering animal stench that grew stronger as he edged toward the shuddering window. Leaning out, he couldn't believe his eyes. Like a dark brown raging torrent, hundreds of cattle flooded by, rampaging up the street. Broad-shouldered and bony brutes, their big heads carried horns as wide as a man's outstretched arms and looked like the tangled, twisted branches of upwrenched trees being swept along by a furious brown flood. Awed, he gasped, "Longhorns."

He'd heard so much about them! There'd been stories concerning them in the New York newspapers and magazines, but he'd put down what he'd read of them as the writers' wild exaggerations. Now, here they were surging below him in the flesh, as true-to-life and fearsome as the stories promised. On their way east toward the railroad corrals with the blazing sun beating down on them and glinting from the points of those formidable horns, they were half an hour passing before he saw the handful of cowboys who were driving them. Lithe and limber astride their horses as they emerged from a thick, trailing cloud of brown dust, they seemed more like the Four Horsemen of the Apocalypse than mortals.

"That was part of the Colter herd that arrived yesterday from Goliad, Texas," explained Marsh Murdock a few minutes later at the *Eagle.*

"Only part of it?" asked Tyrone, incredulously.

"What you saw was about a thousand head. The rest of them, about seven thousand, are pastured about three miles to the west of town. The ones you observed have been sold to a livestock dealer from Kansas City and are being shipped out already. Buck Colter's B-C brand's well known for quality, so there'll be no problem selling the remainder, I'm sure."

"I'd like to meet this Buck Colter. Do you happen to know him?"

"Only by reputation, but I'm afraid you won't be meeting him. He was killed recently in a raid against a gang of cattle thieves from across the Rio Grande in Mexico. I ran a story about it, sent by a correspondent in San Antonio. Colter's daughter's running the ranch now but it's her trail boss who handles the drive, a fella by the name of Morgan. He was quite a well-known character in Kansas before he lit out for Texas. I understand he's an old buddy of Charlie Carew's, so I expect you'll run into him if you hang around Long Charlie's saloon this evening."

"I think I'll do just that. Meantime, I'm off to Arnold's Stable to see a man about acquiring some transportation."

By two o'clock, he'd bought a horse the color of the one he'd seen the Indian riding in his mad, losing race with the train. Naming it Redskin for its hue and in memory of the Indian, he bought a saddle and all the rigging and arranged to keep everything at Arnold's Stable, paying a month in advance.

Thirty minutes later at the New York Clothing Emporium he purchased three plain blue shirts, two pairs of jeans, a belt and a brown broad-brimmed, shade-giving Stetson hat with a creased crown.

At three o'clock he had a pair of ready-made boots that fit perfectly and had him walking an inch taller.

Studying himself in the mirror in his hotel room, he was satisfied, but at dinner in the crowded dining room he felt a rising sense of awkwardness and a suspicion that he was being laughed at that gnawed at him until he pushed through the green doors of Long Charlie's Saloon when Carew greeted him by bellowing, "Well gawd a'mighty, you look like you was born in these parts. That's a mighty fine outfit, yessiree. I'd say you was made for them duds. Musta set you back a pretty penny."

Sheepishly, Tyrone replied, "With the boots, almost as much as the horse."

Carew slapped a big hand on the bar. "You purchased a hoss, too? Jesus, you've had yourself a busy day. Acquirin' all that gear, you prob'ly worked up a heck of a thirst. Will it be the Irish agin'?"

"I may change my clothes, Charlie, but I'll never switch my liquor."

Carew poured a brimming shot. "Did you git yourself a gun as well?"

"Nah."

"Well, I'd advise it, my friend. And learn how to shoot it. This is Wichita, Kansas, don't fergit. There's folks here that'd shoot you down as soon as look at you no matter what you're wearin'. And sometimes on account of it. They didn't put up those warnin's about checkin' guns for the fun of it, believe me. I'd hate to see you run afoul of some damned fool cowhand who's got a bellyfull of whiskey, a six-shooter in his mitt and his cap set on makin' you his target practice. Git yourself iron, boy!"

Tyrone gulped the whiskey. "I'll think about it."

"Don't think about it, do it," snapped Carew, topping the glass. "You by yerself tonight?"

"Yeah, but if a fellow named Morgan shows up, be so kind as to point him out to me, will you? I understand he's a pal of yours. Marsh Murdock told me about him. I'd like to meet him."

Carew exploded with enthusiasm. "Morgan? He's my pal all right, from way back. I heard he hit town today but I ain't seen hide or hair of him so far. If Morgan's in Wichita, he's bound to be in, though. There's no way Ole Morg'll skip seein' his old buddy from Abilene. Count on me. If Morgan shows up, I'll give you the high sign."

"I'll be parked in Murdock's usual spot—observing the clientele," said Tyrone, taking the bottle of whiskey with him to the rear of the warm and smoky room.

It was nearly midnight when Carew raised a long arm above the heads of his customers, waving it as he yelled, "Hey, Tyrone. He's here! Morgan's here!"

SIX

Morgan's Story

"You've been hankerin' to meet cowboys, Tyrone," declared Carew. "Well, here's the best there is."

"I can do my own braggin', Charlie," said the slender youth as he lifted himself out of a slouch and thumbed back a nearly shapeless hat to reveal searching cornflower-blue eyes, a lean face with skin suntanned to the tone of fine leather and wisps of pale yellow hair on his upper lip that seemed to be struggling to become a mustache. A red neckerchief underscored a strong, clean-shaven jaw. His shirt had been a dark shade of blue but was bleached by the sun as months in a saddle in all kinds of weather also had blanched worn blue jeans stuffed into the tops of high square-toed, brush-scuffed boots. A black gunbelt around his narrow hips supported a holster emptied of his Colt .45 in compliance with the law.

"I'm told it was your herd passing my hotel that knocked me out of my bed this morning," said Tyrone.

"I apologize for the inconvenience, but, since Charlie tells me you've come to Wichita to write a book about cowboys, I expect any discombobulation at such an early hour must have been offset by the educational experience."

"The sight of hundreds of cattle filling up an entire city street is one I'll never forget, believe me. I hear you've got seven thousand more just outside town."

The leathery face crinkled into a mischievous grin. "Care to buy 'em?"

"I'm afraid the only beef that I'm in the market for is in the form of steaks, one at a time."

"I fancy 'em that way myself. I'm prejudiced, of course, but I believe the choicest steaks come from beef raised with the B-C brand of the Colter ranch of Goliad, Texas. Maybe you'd care to ride out to the range and see 'em eye to eye?"

"If you're sure the sight of me wouldn't spook them . . ."

Sparkling keen blue eyes danced from Tyrone's crisp new hat to his stiff and shiny boots. "You look okay to me."

"Then I'd be pleased to accept your kind invitation. How long will you be in Wichita?"

"As long as it takes to sell off the herd. A few days at least. Could be as long as a month, maybe two. But that's the lot of the cowboy, I guess. It's like being in the army. You hurry up to get somewhere and then you wait."

"What else is it like? Is it dangerous? Fun?"

"A heap of both."

"Describe a typical cowboy for me."

"Some folks might say he's a noisy galoot with bowed legs, a brass belly and his butt in a saddle who hates any kind of work that can't be done in one. I'd say he's just a fella with guts, a hoss and a job to do."

"You'd never know it to look at Morgan now," interjected Carew as he set whiskeys before them, "but the first time I laid eyes on him he was almost as green around the gills as you, Tyrone. This was long before he took to pushin' cattle. Oh, he was a sorry sight the night I picked him up out of the mud after a bunch of card-sharpin' thieves rolled him, six years ago in Abilene."

Morgan groaned. "Charlie, you're not goin' to tell that worn out old yarn?"

"Why not? It's interestin' and instructive. Tyrone, here, might benefit from the tellin'."

"Then I'd better tell it," insisted Morgan. "That way, Tyrone'll get it straight!"

"Suits me," shrugged Carew, folding his arms across his chest like the ungainly wings of a giant bird.

"I was a kid who got played for a sucker," said Morgan with a swipe of a thumb at his boyish mustache. "I was fresh from a couple of years with George Armstrong Custer's Seventh Cavalry at Fort Riley and on my way to California. When I stopped for the night at Abilene, I got tricked into thinkin' I'd won a bundle of money fair and square in a card game in the town's only saloon at that time. But it was just a plan by the three of 'em to see how much money I had on me. They let me win and after I left the saloon, they banged me over the head and robbed me! I was young and foolish. End of story."

"The hell it is," boomed Carew, unlimbering his great arms. "Tell what happened later."

Morgan frowned and toyed with his whiskey glass. "Leave it be, Charlie."

"The man's lookin' for things to write about in a book!"

"What happened later?" pleaded Tyrone.

Morgan drank the whiskey in a gulp. "Let him tell it."

"It was a year or so after," said Carew excitedly. "The three who pulled that dirty trick on Morgan—a trio of brothers named the Dowds—rode into Abilene again, showin' up at my establishment where they tried pullin' their little scheme on a young, drunk Texas cowhand. Morgan was there but they didn't recognize him. Well, Morg remembered them, saw what they was plannin' and promptly prevented 'em from carryin' out their scheme . . . by way of pluggin' all three. It was a big thing at the time. It made Morgan famous. Newspapers took to callin' him the Gun Man of Abilene."

"It was very embarrassing," muttered Morgan. "The whole thing got blown up by a goddamned newspaperman. Sorry! I understand you're one of the breed. I got nothin' personal against newspapermen. Fact is, I've got a good friend who operates a paper in Abilene. Name of Hank Kidder. Know him?"

"Never been to Abilene."

"I hear it's not what it used to be."

"There was nobody there better with a Colt pistol," asserted Carew. "In fact, Morg's just the fella to advise you on outfittin' yourself with a six-shooter and to show you how to use it properly."

"I'm sure Morgan has more important things to do with his time than instruct me in how to use a pistol," replied Tyrone. "Besides, I haven't made up my mind about getting one."

"I've been tryin' to convince him to get himself a firearm for protection," said Carew urgently.

"Charlie's right about that," said Morgan.

"There's just no gettin' around it," nodded Carew as he topped Morgan's empty glass.

"If you're gonna purchase a gun," said Morgan, "I'll be glad to accompany you to the gunsmith's."

"That's kind of you. Tomorrow? Come round to my hotel and I'll buy you breakfast first."

SEVEN

Lessons

"I'd say you got yourself a mighty good deal on that hoss," judged Morgan as Tyrone led Redskin out of the barn.

Flattered, Tyrone broke into a grin. "Yeah, not bad for a city boy, if I do say so myself."

"Not bad for anybody," said Morgan. "That's a fine saddle, too. Seein's how well you've done so far, I'd say that you and the West are goin' to get along fine, Tyrone; just fine. All you need to complete your outfittin' is . . ."

Tyrone rubbed a hand against his right hip. "I know! A shooting iron!"

"I was goin' to say 'a wipe,' " said Morgan, grinning and lifting the tail of his neckerchief and flicking it like a horse's tail. "You wear 'em round your neck until you have to put 'em across your mouth to keep the trail dust out. You also use 'em to mop the sweat off your face." His hand dropped to his side. "But, yeah, you do look sort of naked without a six-gun hangin' to your frame," he said, deftly unholstering his. "This here's a Colt Army forty-four. Had it since the War."

"Used it a lot?"

Morgan's eyes turned toward the ground. Digging dirt with his toe, he said, "Only in self-defense." The blue eyes shifted up as Tyrone climbed into his new saddle. "I know Charlie Carew's prob'ly got you all riled up with all that bullshit about me and my artistry with a gun. Pardon the salty language."

"I've heard worse."

Morgan slipped the Colt into its holster. "You mean it's not all gentlemanly conversation back in New York?"

"Hardly."

Morgan vaulted onto his blue-black horse. "Now let's go see about gettin' you a suitable firearm, compadre."

"Compadre?"

"That's Mexican lingo, meanin' friend, pal, buddy," said Morgan, booting his horse toward the gate of the corral. "Down in South Texas there's a lot of Mexicans. You hang around Mexicans, you get to talkin' like 'em. But right now, you and I are goin' to palaver the lingo of Mr. Sam Colt."

"Who's he?"

Morgan laughed. "The great equalizer!"

Mr. Raymond Geraty, gunsmith, was a tall, talkative man who kept up on his trade. "There's a brand new Colt comin' this way this year," he said enthusiastically as Morgan examined the wares laid out for them. "It's gonna be a .45 single action six-gun that takes center-fired cartridges and I hear-tell it's a beauty. Not that the ones you're lookin' at aren't fine examples of the gunmaker's craft, of course. You can't go wrong for the price, but if the cost of a new one is too steep, I've got some dandy re-builts."

"We're only interested in the new," said Tyrone.

"Try this one for fit," smiled Morgan. "It's a Colt Pocket Navy, .38 centerfire with a blued five-and-half inch barrel and checkered walnut grip for a firm grasp."

"Say, you know your firearms, sir," exclaimed the gunsmith.

Cracking a smile, Tyrone whispered, "I trust so, you being the Gun Man of Abilene."

"We'll want a belt and a right-sized holster; a second-hand one if you got it," said Morgan to the gunsmith. "Second-hand in a holster's fine, if it's been properly broken in," he said to Tyrone.

Geraty brought the belt and holster.

"How's that feel in your hand, Tyrone?" asked Morgan. "Satisfyin'?"

"Funny way to put it," said Tyrone, weighing the gun in his palm, "but, yeah—quite satisfactory."

"Now all you need is some instruction; what somebody once called the Catechism of the Gun. We'll do that someplace where there'll be minimal chance of shootin' somebody you don't mean to. That, by the way, is the first lesson in the Catechism; Never shoot anybody you didn't intend to, startin' with yourself."

Tyrone slid the gun into the supple holster.

"Now that you've taken this big step on the way to your conversion to the ways of the West, how'd you like to accompany me while I ride out to check on my men and cattle?" asked Morgan. "After that, you can get some practice handlin' your new six-shooter."

Strapping on the gun, Tyrone beamed. "Sounds good to me, compadre."

Outside, he felt as he had when he'd first put on his new clothes and boots—as if everyone were looking at him, but in the growing heat of the morning on Main Street, no one paid any mind to him.

"That newspaperman I mentioned last night tried to talk me into goin' to New York once," said Morgan as they unhitched their horses. "He had the idea that I could become a newspaperman myself. But I was young and foolish and feelin' the tug of the frontier, so here I am eight years later pushin' longhorns."

"Lots of folks think that's pretty exciting and romantic."

"Oh, it has its moments." He laughed as he poked his horse into a gallop with Tyrone coming along capably on Redskin.

Presently, they reached the herd, drawing to a stop on an elevating bump of ground.

"Wow," exclaimed Tyrone. "The good Lord must love cattle to have made so many of them."

As they rode on and approached the herd, the men tending them looked lean and tough with sun-weathered skin, tight lips, set jaws and searching eyes.

"Here comes somebody," said Tyrone, nodding toward an approaching rider.

"That's my caporal, Felipe Hidalgo, my right hand man, known as Dalgo for short. If it's cowpunchin' you want to know about, Dalgo's the one to talk to."

"Buenos dias, boss," grinned the Mexican, drawing up. "Who's this? The buyer for the herd?"

"Afraid not, *amigo.* Tyrone here is only interested in getting his beef one plate at a time. How are things in camp?"

"Very fine, boss. Except for the hot weather, nothin' to worry about."

"And the men? How are they holdin' up?"

Dalgo stroked his large mustache. "They can smell the town. They're anxious to get the herd sold and to have their wages. You know how they feel. You was one of 'em."

At nightfall, Tyrone settled cross-legged next to Morgan at the edge of a campfire as the men of the Colter ranch went about their business with silent lips and searching glances, giving him a wide berth. "I guess they're wondering about me, eh?" he asked Morgan.

"For three months they've been a world unto themselves," explained Morgan to Tyrone at his side. "It becomes an instinct. If someone new shows up in their midst they get a little standoffish. They're like a family. Each knows that his well-being and that of the herd rests upon the man on the next horse, from the two point drivers to the swing riders on opposite sides of the herd to those at the drag end. From start to finish they have to be a team working for the good of the herd and the boss who owns it because if they're to reap the rewards of their labors when they come to the end of the trail, their boss must prosper. So, you see, they've done all the work and now it's up to me to see that it all pays off. The whole thing comes down to the bargaining I'll be doing day after tomorrow with some Chicago livestock men at the Munger House."

"Big responsibility," said Tyrone. "Are you nervous about it?"

"A little, but right now I've got somethin' to keep my mind off it."

"What could that be?"

Morgan grinned. "Why, teachin' you how to shoot without gettin' either of us killed in the process."

For that purpose in the morning he chose a hollow far away from the herd. "Don't want no stampedes, do we?" he said as they rode into the shallow, grassy bowl. "Before you do any shootin'," he went on as they dismounted, "I'm goin' to recite the Catechism of the Gun as drummed into me by Mr. Virgil Coggins of Junction City when he was teachin' me to handle a gun in what he called Kansas Style. The first rule is Respect. Always respect that firearm hangin' from your hip. You payin' attention?"

"Sure am."

"You'd better be, 'cause it may save your life someday," said Morgan, drawing his Colt. "The second rule is one which I just broke. Only draw your gun if you intend to shoot it. And when do you shoot? Only if you intend to kill. Never shoot to wound. A wounded man can still kill you. Got it?"

"Draw only to shoot to kill."

"Right, but that doesn't mean you do it in a hurry. Never hurry. When it comes to guns, a man who's in a hurry soon winds up in his grave. It's not the speed that matters; it's accuracy."

"Draw only to shoot to kill and don't be in a hurry, be accurate. Is that it?"

"Not quite. Now let's consider why you'd be drawin' on a man in the first place. Unless you're a crazy man who just goes around killin' for the sake of killin', there must be a reason for you to be unleashing that gun of yours. Now what would that reason be? Provocation. A decent and righteous man will use his six-gun against another man only when sorely provoked. There's a danger in that. The danger of bein' so riled that you forget all the rules of the Catechism. So, the Golden Rule of the Gun is that you must never lose your head. Like everything else in life, the proper use of a gun begins in the head. If you can keep your head when provoked, you'll probably live to tell about it. Think then shoot. Head before hand. Got it?"

"Right."

"Now as to the draw. You want the gun to slip into your hand easily from the holster. Get yourself some ties to anchor the bottom to your thigh. Don't wear your belt too high. You should strap it on so that the butt of the gun is even with the butt of your hand."

Tyrone adjusted his belt. "Like this?"

"Looks good," said Morgan. "But try drawin' it."

Tyrone drew the gun easily. "I see what you mean."

"Now as to stance," said Morgan, stepping to Tyrone's side. "I'm gonna show you the Virgil Coggins triangle. You see, the secret to steady shootin' is to minimize the gun's kick. You can do that by holding the gun in both hands." He stepped aside, drawing his Colt and making it the point of the triangle of his forward stretched arms. "Watch my hands as I shoot." He fired once. "See? Hardly any kick at all, allowing you to fire again almost immediately." He fired again. "Now you try it. From the draw."

Tyrone drew easily, took the stance and fired twice.

"Now we'll try it with some targets," said Morgan, striding to his horse and removing an assortment of empty bottles and tin cans which he aligned on an outcropping of rock. "They're a lot smaller than a man, but, of course, they won't be movin' or shootin' back, will they?"

"I trust not," said Tyrone, grinning.

"Have at 'em," said Morgan, hunkering down to watch the first six shots of which four were hits. "Not bad," he said, settling to the ground and sitting cross-legged and silent as his pupil set up the targets and reloaded, repeating the process through the afternoon.

By dusk he was hitting all the targets consistently.

Having said nothing for more than an hour, Morgan rose at last. "That'll do it for today. You're gettin' the hang of it. All you need now is practice. And I pray that's all you'll ever be doin' with that new gun of yours. But if you have to shoot at a man, aim for his belly. Hittin' him there will stop him for sure even if it doesn't kill him outright. Once you've stopped him, the killin' will be easy. And once you've killed one man, killin' the next is easier. Then it just keeps on gettin' easier. The lesson in that, my friend, is . . . don't kill the first one."

"It's too late for that, I'm afraid," said Tyrone, remembering Crazy Sid. "I have killed one man."

"Ah."

"It was strictly self-defense," Tyrone blurted. "You could even say it was an accident!"

"Well let's hope and pray that the poor soul was your last," said Morgan, mounting his horse. "What's your pleasure now? Are you headin' back to town or are you feelin' up to another night of roughin' it one more night in our camp?"

Tyrone beamed. "Oh, your camp, of course!"

EIGHT

Augurin'

A Chinese cook brought their supper on tin plates.

"Chan calls this mess Slumgullion Stew," said Morgan. "Don't ask what's in it."

"If I lucky, it be poison," giggled Chan. "Then Colter Ranch get new boss, better one who not be pain in ass pickin' on cook alla time."

The Slumgullion was tangy beef stew. "This is pretty good stuff, Chan," shouted Tyrone.

"Geez-uz," groaned Morgan, glancing across the campfire at the beaming cook. "Don't tell him that. If you go around praisin' his chow there'll be no livin' with 'im."

Surveying the cowboys as they ate their meal, Tyrone muttered, "The men seem pretty quiet."

Morgan studied them. "Don't mind that. Once they're sure about you, they'll be in an augurin' mood and then you won't be able to shut 'em up."

"Augurin'?"

"That means talkin'. But until these boys have taken the measure of the man behind a new face they're pretty quiet. Don't let it bother you. That's how they treated me at first. The drive that year was run by a man named

Andy Stoner, but called Novillero. There's a man you could've written a book about, if you'd known him. Rangy, flat-bellied, slim-hipped, eagle-eyed and, of course, tight-lipped! He was hard-boiled and firm but he was also fair, honest, fearless, willin' to do anythin' he asked one of his men to do and better at doin' any of the jobs on the drive than anyone under him."

"Sounds admirable."

"The best."

"How come he's not on this drive?"

Morgan gazed blankly into the fire. "He got killed in a stampede."

"Ah. Sorry to hear it."

"On that first drive, he didn't speak to me for nearly a week; he just watched me, measured me. When he made up his mind that I could cut the mustard, he opened up. All the rest followed suit. Then he taught me all there is to know about the cattle game. He called it his 'Cow College.' It was mind-bogglin', believe me; all in a lingo that was half-Spanish, half-American: *orejano, mocho, cimmaron, toro,* critters, yearlin's, bulls, steers, she stuff for females and heavy stuff for pregnant cows, weaners, doggies, leppies, acorn calves, poddies, kettle-bellies, slabsides, slat-ribs, scalawags, cutbacks, brush splitters and mavericks. I learned *bueno* meant "good" and *sabinas* was a color—red and white peppered and splotchy—and how to tell the difference between a brindle, a brockle, a lineback and yeller bellies. And he showed me how to read men as well as cows."

Tyrone looked toward the men finishing their stew, their only sound the scraping of spoons on plates. "That's what they're doing? Reading me?"

"Probably they're hoping you're a buyer," chuckled Morgan, setting aside his empty plate.

"How does Dalgo fit in?"

"He's the caporal. My right-hand man. He's got a darned good yarn he could tell about himself—and prob'ly will; Dalgo was never one for a buttoned lip! His full name is Felipe Hidalgo and he's been like one of the Colter family since he was a kid. He was an orphan that Buck just took in the way you might pick up a stray dog. He was maybe six or seven years old at the time. His old man was a cattle thief that Buck Colter hanged down by the Nueces when he caught him trying to change the Colter brand. It was only after he strung up the thief that Buck discovered he had a kid with him. Dalgo spoke no English at the time and there was no way of knowin' where he'd come from or who his mother was or anything else that would help Buck get the kid back to his kinfolk, so he just took him back to Goliad and handed him over to a woman in town to take care of. Of course, Buck paid the costs. Then, when the kid was grown up a little more, Buck gave him a job. He's been wranglin' Colter cattle ever since."

With the startling suddenness of an apparition, the caporal loomed above them. "That was quite a racket you was makin' all afternoon," he said, grinning down at them.

"Just teachin' Tyrone a little triggernometry," said Morgan.

"None better to be taught by," said the Mexican. "Did he happen to tell you about his own triggernometry while cleanin' out the Juan Flores gang down at Las Cuevas?"

"Not a word," said Tyrone.

"Ah, now there's a story!"

Morgan shot to his feet. "Dalgo," he barked, "ain't you got work to do? Puttin' out the nightriders, for instance?"

"Sure, boss," said the startled Mexican, backing away. "Sure."

"Then, *buenos noches, amigo.*"

"Hasta mañana, boss," said Dalgo, scampering off.

"What's this about Las Cuevas?" insisted Tyrone.

"It's nothin'," said Morgan, busying himself with making up his bed. "We cleaned out some bandidos; Mexican cattle thieves who were holed up across the border from Eagle Pass. That's where Buck Colter got killed. I'd just as soon not talk about it tonight. It's much too pretty a night for such things." He stretched out on the bed with his head cradled in his hands and his eyes peering straight up. "Look at all those stars! Ever see stars like that in New York City?"

"No, I don't think I ever did," said Tyrone. He was standing, his neck craned and his eyes on the sky but his thoughts were fixed on a place called Las Cuevas that he feared this puzzling trail boss named Morgan would never agree to discuss.

Smoking a cheroot and not ready to sleep, Dalgo was happy to talk. "Ah, *señor,*" he began, "Las Cuevas is some story!"

A year ago, it was, he said.

Morgan had led a posse of Nueces Strip ranchers to clean out a gang of cattle thieves whose leader was the notorious Juan Flores.

"They was hidin' out in a box canyon due west of Piedras Negras just across the Rio Grande from Eagle Pass. Morgan and Novillero scouted out the place and saw that it was the perfect layout for an ambush. So Morgan divided the posse into thirds. Novillero was the leader of one group. A rancher named Shanghai Pierce had the second. Morgan and Buck Colter took the rest, includin' me. It was a complete surprise. I can still hear Buck Colter chargin' into that canyon yellin' '*Venceremos!*' from the back of his big gray horse, shootin' from side to side. But then one of the Flores gang rushed out from behind a boulder and shot Buck twice at point blank range. When Morgan saw it, he rode his horse right into that son of a bitch, jumped down and knifed him with a Bowie, again and again. I thought he was never goin' to stop. Countin' that poor bastard, there was twenty-six of the Flores gang killed and seven captured alive. We didn't know which one was Flores or whether he was dead or one of the captured ones, so Morgan made the seven kneel and then passed along the line, stoppin' in front of each of 'em askin', 'Are you Juan Flores?' "

A natural story-teller, Dalgo paused dramatically, puffing on his cigar.

"Of course, none said he was Flores," he continued. "Then Morgan turns to Shanghai Pierce and says, 'This is like *Hamlet.* Do you know your Shakespeare?' Then he says, 'Hamlet's trouble was that he couldn't make up his mind.' And with that he yells, 'I'm not Hamlet,' and side-steps down the line of them prisoners, shootin' each one in the head. When he's done, he walks away sayin', 'And so I am revenged,' which I learned was also words from that play *Hamlet.*"

"Good God," whispered Tyrone. "Seven men executed while he recites Shakespeare!"

"They deserved it," said Dalgo, flipping his smoked-down cheroot into the waning campfire. "They was cattle thieves. And puttin' 'em all together they still wasn't near the worth of Buck Colter, believe me. You're new to these parts, Tyrone, so you might not see the justice in that. But if you stay out here long enough, you will. As to Morgan, he's the best. There's not a man in this camp who wouldn't follow him anywhere he wanted to go. And not a man-jack among 'em who wouldn't do for him what he did for Buck Colter if it came to that."

In the morning as they rode toward Wichita for a ten o'clock meeting with cattle buyers at the Munger House, Morgan looked sidelong at Tyrone, declaring, "Dalgo told you the story of what happened at Las Cuevas, eh?"

"Does it upset you? If it riles you, blame me, not Dalgo. I sort of twisted his arm."

Morgan blurted a laugh. "That little Mexican fart didn't

need any arm twistin'! And no, it doesn't upset me. I've gotten used to bein' talked about. Morgan, the Gun Man of Abilene! Morgan, the Executioner of Las Cuevas! To twist a line from Shakespeare's *Hamlet,* 'O God! Morgan, what a wounded name!' "

At ten at the Munger House, livestock buyers from a Chicago syndicate took the entire Colter herd at twenty dollars a head. In celebration, Morgan bought lunch for Tyrone at noon at the Harris House. At two, Tyrone accompanied Morgan to the Wichita National Bank to draw sufficient cash to pay the Colter cowboys. At dusk, the first of them thundered into Wichita ready to rip.

Not since he was fifteen and witnessing the wild celebrations that erupted in New York City on the night of the day that the news was flashed from Appomattox Court House that Lee had surrendered his sword to Grant, thus ending the Civil War, had Tyrone observed such jubilant tumult in the streets as the rollicking which Morgan's men and those of four other Texas ranches gave to Delano. But unlike that memorable night in April 1865 when he'd been a part of the boisterousness—and as drunk as any soldier—on this sultry summer night in 1873 he was a sober observer, as objective as he could be, drawing on his training as a reporter to coolly note and remember for recording in his notebooks.

NINE

On the Prod

The events of the next night would be recorded in the historical annals of Wichita and Tyrone's notebook as the Battle of Red Beard's Dance Hall.

Blue uniforms dotted the motley flow of Main Street as he rode into town with Morgan. "Looks like an invasion," he joked.

"They're a troop of George Armstrong Custer's Seventh Cavalry," explained Morgan, his eyes on the flapping blue and gold guidon at the head of the double column. "I rode with that outfit when I was a greenhorn kid fresh to Kansas."

"It can't have been that long ago," said Tyrone. "You're not so old, you know."

Stroking his sparse mustache, Morgan cracked a grin behind his hand. "I'm a lot older than I thought I'd be at this age."

Tyrone was watching the passing parade. "Recognize any old saddle buddies?"

"Nah, these men are all since my time," Morgan shrugged.

"What was your rank at the time?"

"I wasn't in the army then, though I'd been in Custer's cavalry during the war. When the Seventh was organized up at Fort Riley soon after the war, I was taken on by Custer as a civilian assistant to the chief of scouts. My boss was Major Hank Kimball, since dead, killed in a battle with Black Kettle's Indians at the Washita in '68. It was after that travesty that I quit soldierin' and headed down to Texas to try my hand at the cattle game."

"At which you've succeeded admirably!"

Morgan jerked his chin toward the horse soldiers. "This looks like a routine patrol takin' advantage of bein' near Wichita for a little rest and recreation." He snorted a laugh. "I know how they feel, believe me."

The sight of the soldiers must have had a powerful effect on Morgan, Tyrone decided, because the moment they'd propped themselves at Long Charlie's bar, Morgan opened up concerning his time with Custer during the war and after.

The hapless individual with the distinction of being the first to be shot by him, said Morgan somberly, had been a golden-haired youth in the butternut and gray uniform of the Confederacy. "I wasn't even a soldier," he said soulfully as his blue eyes opened wide in wonder. "I was fourteen! The kid I killed wasn't much more than that. It happened while the Rebs were stumbling into Union troops in what soon became the Battle of Gettysburg. This stupid young Reb stumbled into a woods above Willoughby Creek and right into my sights. I had a deer rifle." He paused, then added hoarsely, "Imagine killing a man with a deer rifle?"

The Reb had fired first, he asserted clearly. "But I fired true."

Since that unexpected encounter with death only a few miles from the farm where he had been raised by a devout mother and a worldly father, he continued, he'd dealt out a lot of death to others. There'd been enemy soldiers during the war, Cheyenne Indians during expeditions with George Armstrong Custer's Seventh Cavalry patrolling out of Fort Riley and the trio of robbers whose punishment with three shots in a dark alley from his Colt Army revolver made him famous as the Gun Man of Abilene and gave Charlie Carew a favorite tale to tell when augurin' with trail-thirsty cowboys.

"Then came John Redus," he said bitterly.

"Who was he?" asked Tyrone.

"Another foolish owlhoot on the prod."

"On the prod?"

" 'On the prod' means 'lookin' for trouble,' " said Morgan, sipping his liquor. "Redus brought three buddies, also on the prod, and I was their target. This happened in the saloon Charlie had on Texas Street up in Abilene. I killed them all. Bang, bang, bang, bang—just like that. Self-defense, it was. There was no question about that. At least a dozen witnesses saw the four of them going for their guns first. But as fair and honest as the shootings were and with all the testimony acknowledging that I'd been provoked, Joseph McCoy, who rightly was looking out for and protecting the best interests of Abilene and was gravely concerned about the town's growing reputation for lawlessness, suggested that the time had come for me to be moving on."

"That seems unfair," said Tyrone.

"It wasn't for any personal reason that Joe told me to leave. It was just good business. The man had labored long and hard to build the cattle trade at Abilene and could not be faulted for worryin' when things happened that reflected badly upon it. As God had decreed that there was no room in Eden for Cain after he had slain his brother Abel, Joe McCoy decreed there could be no place in Abilene for a gun man, even though I was a friend! I can see now that it was the best thing he ever did for me."

"Really? Why is that?"

"He forced me to grow up. He shooed me down to Texas where I got a job from Buck Colter and learned the cattle trade from Novillero and Dalgo. Instead of me winding up another corpse on the owlhoot trail, I wound up marryin' Buck's daughter, name of Rebecca, and now I'm soon to be a papa. I may already be and just don't know it yet."

Tyrone lifted his Irish whiskey in a toast. "Congratulations!"

"So you see, once upon a time I was just like those horse soldiers. And once upon a time I was just like the cowboys who now work for me. That's why I can say from personal knowledge that with all those cavalrymen and all these bronc busters thrown together, there's bound to be a hot time in the old town of Wichita tonight!"

Adjoining Long Charlie's, Red Beard's dance hall was a long frame building with a hall and bar in front and sleeping rooms in the rear for the convenience of half a dozen prostitutes supervised by Beard's mistress, Josephine McDermitt, a buxom no-nonsense woman who kept tabs on the occupancy of the tiny rooms and made sure the girls split the income earned therein with the owner.

How the trouble that became known as the War at Big Red's started was unclear but that it had been over one of the girls and involved a horse soldier and a Colter cowboy, each claiming rights to the girl known as K.C. because she'd come from Kansas City, was not in dispute.

The trouble was signaled to Tyrone and Morgan having a friendly game of blackjack with the crash of a chair against a wall shared by Charlie's and Red's. Startled but unconcerned, Tyrone said, "I guess you were right about the hot time in the old town."

In contrast to Tyrone as he laid down the deck he was shuffling, Morgan was a study in worry. "Will you excuse me, please?" he said, rising. "I believe some of my men may be next door. I'd better have a look. No stackin' the deck while I'm gone!"

Tyrone lurched to his feet. "Hey, I'm coming with you."

Outside, Morgan glanced at the horses tied up to Red's hitching post. "Yep, I was afraid of this," he said. "Three of those mounts are from the Colter remuda. The rest are army."

The noise pouring from Red's was now riotous.

"Cripes!" said Morgan, rushing toward the dance hall's bright red batwing doors, "I hope my boys aren't in it."

Following Morgan, Tyrone was swept with memories of saloon brawls in New York. "Just like home," he muttered as he entered, trying to stifle a laugh at the scramble made by a dozen soldiers and as many cowboys throwing punches, kicking legs and hurling furniture, all punctuated by girls screaming both in terror and encouragement as Red Beard and his mistress stood aside, helpless.

Leaping upon tangled battlers and wrenching Colter cowboys away from Custer's soldiers, Morgan yelled, "Break it up, break it up, break it up," only to witness the separated fighters pairing off again or with different opponents.

Then, deafeningly, three shots rang out and the effect was, Tyrone noted, the same as a bell being rung at the end of a round of prize fighting. The fighters drifted away from the center of the room as if they were withdrawing to their corners, creating a widening circle.

In its center, a cavalryman lay dead, shot through the heart. Two others writhed near him, wounded.

Moments later, the batwings swung open, admitting Mike Meagher, the marshal of Wichita, a broad-shouldered, granite-jawed and hard-eyed assertion of law and order that made a silver-colored star on his chest appear needless. "All right, let's sort this mess out," he ordered, his face contorted with disgust. "Army on that side of the room, cowhands on t'other. Nobody leaves the place until I've had a look at all the firearms you may possess to see which of 'em was just fired."

Slowly, as the investigation progressed, Morgan's three cowboys were cleared.

When the last of them was judged innocent of any shooting, Meagher turned to Morgan. "I gather that those fellas work for you?"

"They do."

"Well, given the touchy nature of things as they now stand, I suggest you order them back to wherever you've set up your camp and to stay there until these army boys have moved on."

"Our business is done here in Wichita anyway," said Morgan, "so I expect they'll be headin' back to Texas pronto."

"Tomorrow is not too soon," said the marshal.

Returned to Charlie's, fueled by Irish whiskey and animated by their vivid memories of the battle next door, Tyrone and Morgan resumed playing blackjack, assuming the trouble was behind them, but at midnight a spindly Colter cowboy Tyrone knew as Hector barged in and grabbed Morgan's arm. "You gotta come quick, boss."

Slamming down his cards, Morgan groaned. "Now what?"

"Dalgo's in a heap of trouble," blurted Hector, frowning. "You gotta come and help him."

Morgan grimaced. "What the hell did he do?"

"He got drunk and wound up in a knife fight at a bawdy house over in Delano."

Morgan shot to his feet. "Dalgo was knifed?"

"No, boss," giggled Hector, "it was Dalgo that did the knifin'."

"Christ," grunted Tyrone.

"Where is he?" demanded Morgan.

"The law's tossed him into the calaboose, boss."

Morgan turned to Charlie Carew. "Where's the marshal's office?"

"Top end of the street," said Carew with a nod in the general direction.

Morgan rushed for the door.

"Mind if I come along?" asked Tyrone, catching up.

"You thrive on disaster, don't you?"

"I know I just met Dalgo," said Tyrone, feeling wounded by the remark, "but I feel as if he's a compadre already."

"Sure," said Morgan, punching the batwings. "C'mon."

Seated behind an oak desk facing the door and bending over a bowl of stew, Meagher looked up sharply and moaned, "You again?"

"I believe you've got one of my men in here," said Morgan.

"Seems everywhere your men go in this town, trouble follows." Wary eyes shifted to the gun strapped to Morgan's hip. "There's an ordinance about wearin' iron within city limits, Morgan. Dischargin' a gun in town is punishable by a twenty-five dollar fine." The eyes drifted to Tyrone's pistol. "Same applies to you, fella. Didn't you see the sign about guns at the bridge? Or can't you boys read?"

"Only sign I saw was the one put up by my pal Charlie Carew," replied Morgan, striding to the desk.

Meagher grunted. "That cussed thing." He shook his head ruefully. "That damned billboard has caused me more trouble than I'd care to think about. Long Charles is a friend of yours, eh?"

"Since way back."

"Way back where?"

"Abilene."

Meagher's eyes narrowed to slits. "You're *the* Morgan? I didn't put you and the name together."

"The only name I care about is Felipe Hidalgo. Is he here?"

Meagher nodded slowly. "In a cage."

"May I know the charge?"

"He knifed another Mexican in a brawl in the parlor of Ida May's bawdy house down by the bridge. Why is it that your men always wind up in brawls, Morgan?"

"Is the man he knifed dead?"

"He ought to be but he ain't."

"So the charge against Dalgo is what? Assault?"

"The charge ain't fixed yet. He's only in on suspicion. Right now there's nobody who's willin' to say exactly what happened. Just like in that mess over at Red's. Never saw so many tight lips in one night in my life! If the victim croaks, then it'll be a murder case and maybe lips will be looser. Meantime, I've tossed him in the pokey just to keep him from being killed by the pals of the Mex he stuck. Protective custody."

"When might I post bail for his release?"

"Stop by here on your way back to Texas and I'll spring him. That is if the Mexicano he cut doesn't die."

"Can I talk to Dalgo now?"

"Sure," said Meagher, rising behind the desk and reaching for a loop of keys. "The cage is in the next room. But leave that Colt Army iron of yours here on my desk."

Laying the gun on the oak with a heavy thump, Morgan said, "Suspicious soul, aren't you?"

"Suspicion is the only life insurance policy I carry."

"Don't know how long this will take," said Morgan, turning to Tyrone. "No use your hangin' around. I'll catch up with you at Charlie's as soon as I can."

"Sure," said Tyrone, wheeling around to leave.

"Just a minute," snapped the marshal, pointing to

Tyrone's hip. "Better check your gun, too, mister. Unless you're leavin' town, also."

Tyrone surrendered the gun.

Meagher studied it. "Brand new, eh?"

"Yep."

Meagher sniffed the muzzle. "Recently fired."

"Practicing."

Depositing the gun in a drawer and handing Tyrone a metal claim check, Meagher said, "I hope that's all you ever do with it."

If ever there were somebody worth putting in a book, Morgan seemed to be him, thought Tyrone gleefully as he strode toward Long Charlie's. With a laugh, he thought, "I've even got the title: *The Gun Man of Abilene.*"

He did not see Morgan again that night, but ideas for a book about him were still popping into his head late the next morning when he walked into Long Charlie's looking for him. "You missed him," announced Carew, bringing the bottle of Irish whiskey. "He collected that Mexican of his bright 'n' early this mornin' and headed back down the trail. He'd've said goodbye to you but with rumors that friends of the fella that got knifed was comin' lookin' for the Mexican, and in view of last night's riot at Red's, well, Morg figured it best that he and his men skeedaddle."

"Can't blame him for that, I suppose," said Tyrone.

"He did tell me to tell you that it was a pleasure to have met you and that he wishes you success with the book you'll be writin'," said Carew, "only please don't put him in it. Of course, if you make up your mind to do so, I can provide plenty of stories about him."

"Thanks, Charlie, but I'll respect the man's wishes."

TEN

Death Deals a Hand

When Morgan was a two-week old memory, on a sultry afternoon in July, Tyrone took up a position at Long Charlie's bar and observed that taking part in a four-handed poker game in progress at the rear of the room were the cousins who'd been pointed out to him on the train. "The Ludlums sure do believe in starting early," he muttered to Charlie.

"That game's been going on all night," whispered Carew. "How do you come to know the Ludlums?"

"I don't," said Tyrone, lighting a cheroot. "I only know of them by reputation."

"Some rep," said Carew. "My advice is, they're best avoided."

"I didn't come way out here from New York to avoid meeting folks, Charlie."

Carew frowned. "Are you fixin' to get into that game?"

"I'm just taking the advice of an old friend by the name of Ben Turner," Tyrone answered, lurching away from the bar. " 'A faint heart never filled a flush.' "

Playing with the Ludlums were a fat young man wearing fancy clothes and the expression of a player on his way to being skinned and a lanky fair-haired cowboy whose stack of chips pointed to a streak of good luck.

Squinting at Tyrone through a thin stream of smoke from the cigarette dangling from the right side of his mouth, Mickey Ludlum declared, "You can do one of two things, stranger. You can join the game or you can get lost. We don't fancy kibbitzers. So what'll it be?"

"Deal me in. The name's Tyrone."

"Major Seth Whittier," said the fat man, reaching out for a handshake. Soft-spoken, he sounded Southern. His brown suit was worn with a vest adorned by a heavy gold watch chain.

"I'm Jed Slade," said the cowboy, amiably.

"Names don't matter," growled Moe Ludlum, dealing the cards. "Just ante up, Irish."

The first hand flicked out to Tyrone was a full house and the pot he won was fifteen dollars. "Beginner's luck, eh, Major?"

"If somebody else hadn't dealt those cards," said Whittier, "I'd be a little s'picious."

"And rightly so," nodded Tyrone, scooping up the winnings.

Moe passed the deck to his cousin. "We'll see how that beginner's luck holds," Mickey said, dealing.

Tyrone lifted his cards. Fanning them tightly and close to his chest, he swallowed a gasp as he gazed blankly at three kings, a jack and a trey.

"Open," said the major with a gust of smoke and a dollar chip.

Everyone was in.

The major took two cards.

"Three," said the cowboy with a telling grimace.

Tyrone discarded the trey and picked up the jack of diamonds.

"Dealer takes one," said Mickey Ludlum. "Raise five."

"Out," sighed the major forlornly.

"Me too," said Moe angrily.

"Too rich for me," said the cowboy, tilting on his chair.

"See you and call," said Tyrone flatly.

"They're all red," grinned Mickey, spreading a heart flush on the table.

"Looks like beginner's luck still holds," said Tyrone with a grin as he laid down the full house.

"Criminey," moaned the cowboy, lifting his battered tan hat and scratching unruly blond hair. "How's the man do it?"

"Are we here to talk to ourselves or to play poker?" grumbled Mickey.

"I'm afraid my pocket's as empty as a banker's heart," said the major, pushing away from the table. He drew out his watch, a fine, heavy gold timepiece. "As much as I hate to quit when I'm on a losing streak, I've got business to attend to. I closed a deal on seven thousand head of cattle this morning over at the Harris House and I'm due at the bank; overdue, in fact."

"What about you, Texas?" asked Mickey Ludlum of the cowboy. "You still in?"

"Yeah, I'm game for another couple of hands," he said brightly.

As his cousin watched the major, Moe passed the deck to Tyrone. "Your turn to deal I believe." But two losing hands later he tossed in his cards. "My luck's turned sour. Deal me out."

"Same for me," said his cousin, rising abruptly and making for the door.

"Well, that leaves the two of us," said Tyrone to the cowboy. "Unless you're folding your tent, too."

"Shoot no. I got nothin' better to do. I'm in till the cows come home."

"Sounds good to me," said Tyrone.

Four hands later the cowboy was cleaned out. "Mister, lady luck sure kissed you today," he said, loping toward the exit.

"Appears so," said Tyrone, lazily gathering his winnings.

Five minutes later, Main Street erupted with gunfire.

* * *

Everyone in anywise connected with the livestock trade had come to know the roly-poly and affable Major Seth Whittier of Llano, Texas, to be one of the Lone Star state's most chivalrous cattlemen, having a pleasant word for everyone and ever-ready to do some favor or perform a kind deed—the epitome and embodiment of the Southern gentleman. Born in Charleston, South Carolina, he had witnessed the bombardment of Fort Sumter at the age of eighteen and promptly presented himself to Major General Pierre Gustave Toutant Beauregard, serving the Confederacy with distinction to its last gasp and rising to the rank by which he was addressed after the war.

Still a young man and eager for new adventures, he'd moved to Texas to try his hand at ranching. When Kansas markets opened, he was among the first to drive longhorns northward, earning a reputation for his straightforward business dealings, genial companionship and passionate card playing, accepting losses gracefully.

At the table in Long Charlie's, he'd lost two hundred dollars, a pittance compared to the amount he'd earned by the sale of seven thousand head of beeves.

On his way to the Wichita National Bank he had paused a moment at the offices of his friend Marsh Murdock's *Eagle* with the intention of inviting the editor to be his guest for dinner that evening at the Harris House. "I'm settling my affairs by turning a sizeable draft for the sale of my beeves into cash to pay off my men," he'd explained, rearing back in his chair and drumming pudgy fingers against his generous belly. "Then, first thing tomorrow I'm taking the train to Kansas City to purchase some furnishings for an addition to my house." He toyed with a gold watch chain. "So this is your last chance to tap me for a dinner till next year."

"Seth, there are three basic rules that a newspaperman lives by," replied Murdock. "Never pass by a privy without using it, never stand when you can sit and never turn down a free meal."

With the appetizing prospect of food on his mind, Whittier left Murdock's office, nimbly dodging and weaving the traffic of Main Street and entering the bank just before it was to close its vault for the day.

Fifteen minutes later, he emerged.

Tucked under his right arm, a thick brown envelope contained a cashier's draft for the bulk of the amount he'd obtained for his cattle and two thousand dollars in cash to pay the wages and a generous bonus to the hardy men who'd driven his herd up from Texas and who were waiting for him at the hotel. Never a suspicious man, he did not notice that he had been followed to the bank and from it by Moe Ludlum.

Halfway between the bank and the Harris House, Mickey had waited at the mouth of an alley affording a view of Main Street and, as Whittier passed, he leapt out from the alley, drawing a gun. "Far enough, mister."

The unmistakable muzzle of another gun poked into his back. "Not a peep," whispered Moe from behind. "Just give it up."

"I know you," exclaimed Whittier as Mickey wrenched the envelope from him. "The boys from the card game!"

"You got that right," said Mickey, grinning as he stepped back. "Too bad for you," he laughed, shooting twice into the cattleman's bulging belly.

With a swoop, Moe plucked the dead man's gold watch.

A moment later, he and Mickey galloped northward firing into the air in a racketing fusillade that cleared the street and the sidewalks.

Of the curious who quickly gathered around the corpse, Marshal Meagher asked, "Anybody see this? Anyone know who did it?"

A wide-eyed, gangly boy stepped forward excitedly. "I did! I seen it. The Ludlums done it. They hightailed it on hosses makin' toward the depot."

Even before the shooting had stopped, Tyrone had come

running from Long Charlie's. "Ah, what a damned shame," he blurted. "The man seemed like a hell of a nice fellow."

"One of the best," said Marsh Murdock, peering glumly down at the body.

"How'd you know him?" asked Meagher, addressing Tyrone.

"I only met him a while ago over a game of cards at Charlie's."

"Robbed for his winnings, most likely," said the marshal.

"No," asserted Murdock. "He'd just been to the bank, so the Ludlums probably got thousands."

Meagher shook his head. "I tell these drovers not to go round packin' cash but they never listen. Damned fools." He turned to the boy. "They headed toward the depot, you said?"

"Yep," said the boy, pointing.

Stepping from the crowd, Tyrone asserted, "Marshal, I'm going with you."

"The hell you are," snapped Meagher, striding toward his office. "Trackin' a couple of killers with night comin' on will be tricky enough for me, so it sure ain't no proper place for a city-bred civilian."

"I'm a reporter," said Tyrone emphatically. "As such, I've got a right to go along."

The marshal spun around. "And who gave you that right?"

"It's right there in the Bill of Rights of the Constitution of the United States—a special right spelled out for people like me called Freedom of the Press!"

"Freedom of the . . . ?" Meagher snorted a laugh. "Look, kid, all that stuff might buffalo the coppers in New York, but this is Wichita. In Wichita, I'm the law. And I'm telling you that you do not have the right to get yourself killed chasing outlaws." Entering his office, he banged the door shut.

Slamming it open, Tyrone bellowed, "Marshal, I'm going after the Ludlums, either with you or right behind you."

Strapping on his six-gun, Meagher squinted toward Tyrone's silhouette in the doorway. "Who are the Ludlums to you anyway? You got a personal account to settle with them? Did you come here spouting off about freedom of the press to cover some grudge you're carrying?"

Tyrone strode to the desk. "It's nothing of the kind. Other than liking the fellow who got killed, it's not a personal matter. This is strictly professional. This is a damned good story! I came out here to write about life in the West and I sure as hell have no intention of letting this example of wanton killing pass me by. You've got your duty. I got mine."

Meagher paused, thinking a moment, then cracked a smile. "You're crazy, you know that?"

Tyrone nodded slowly. "Hard-headed-Irishman crazy, that's me."

"Boy, you take the cake!"

"Yes, sir, and I'll also take my gun, thank you," said Tyrone, fishing in his pocket for the round metal claim check and slamming it on the desk. "I've got a right to bear arms, too, you know. It says so in the . . ."

"Yeah! The Bill of Rights!" Pulling open his desk drawer, Meagher withdrew Tyrone's Colt. "Okay. Consider yourself deputized. Here's your gun. Try not to shoot me with it, all right?"

"Promise," chuckled Tyrone, holstering it.

Meagher stabbed a finger into Tyrone's chest. "But get this straight, kid. I call the shots. You do what I say every step of the way. Clear?"

"Absolutely."

"Okay. Now, the Ludlums were seen going north like a pair of bats out of hell, meanin' they'll be followin' the railroad tracks," said Meagher, taking a rifle from a rack. "My guess is they'll be cutting a beeline toward their old stomping grounds around Newton. At the depot I'll send a telegram to the law in Newton to be on the lookout, but if we run across 'em and they set their caps on makin' the matter difficult, don't hesitate to use that bright and shiny new pistol of yours to save Sedgwick County taxpayers the cost of two hangings."

ELEVEN

Born to Die

Five miles due north of the town, the Ludlums' trail veered westward from the railroad tracks, crossing shallow Chisholm Creek and a narrow strip of woodlands and then over the horseneck-deep Arkansas. "Well, the marshal of Newton can forget about my telegram," muttered Meagher. "These boys ain't going home; that's pretty clear. They appear to be making for the buffalo country around Dodge City. They can lose themselves pretty easy amongst the tight-lipped crowd they've got over there."

"How far's that?" asked Tyrone.

"As the crow flies, about a hundred and twenty five miles," said Meagher, studying the failing twilight. "It'll be night soon and no moon. That's not good."

Tyrone shifted in his saddle, creaking with newness. "Does that mean you're calling it quits?"

"Hell no," grunted Meagher, plunging his bay into the river. "The dark gives them an advantage, so they'll keep moving. That means we have to keep going. Trailing 'em will be difficult but not impossible. People think nighttime is totally black, but it isn't. It's shades of gray. Folks think you can't see things in the dark, but you can. Especially outdoors. There's always some light. Quit on account of darkness? Never."

"Good," said Tyrone, smiling and nudging Redskin forward.

"There's little wind," observed Meagher as they rose from the riverbed into high grass. "That's in our favor. If there was wind it would stir the grass and possibly wipe out the signs of their passing." He pointed ahead. "See how the stems are pushed back and aside by their horses plowing through? Only thing better than high grass when you're trailin' a man is deep snow. Let's just hope we don't run into somebody else's trail crossin' theirs. Or buffaloes on the move. Or a cussed herd of Texas cattle churnin' up the grass."

The night fell as Meagher had predicted, dark but not impenetrable, black but not blinding. They moved slowly through it, rocking easily in their saddles as they followed the path of disturbed grass until dawn began as a faint pink blush behind them and the trail turned southerly. "This looks bad," said Meagher. "If they've turned left it means they might've decided to make for the Indian country of the Cherokee Strip. If they reach that hellish place we'll never locate 'em. They might even be aimin' to go all the way to the Mexican border."

"What's the attraction there?"

"The lack of law and if any does show up it's just a quick dash across the Rio Grande and sanctuary in Mexico. Or they might throw in with a hardcase by the name of Saldana who heads a nest of bandits at a spot called Hezekiah."

"How far are you prepared to go after them?"

"I mean to catch them in Kansas, God willin' and the cricks don't rise. All of this, assumin' I didn't lose their track somewhere in the night."

"I'm sure you didn't," said Tyrone emphatically, though he had no way of knowing.

"I appreciate the confidence," said the marshal.

"I only hope having me tagging along didn't hamper you."

Meagher drew rein. "No, you haven't at all been the pain in the ass I expected you to be."

"Neither have you, as a matter of fact," answered Tyrone with a lopsided grin.

The marshal barked a laugh and drew a pair of misshapen cheroots from his shirt pocket. "Do you indulge, Tyrone?"

"Thanks. I've been craving a smoke all night but left mine back at the Harris House."

"I wouldn't've let you have one at night anyway," said Meagher, striking a match on his saddle horn and lighting both.

Tyrone sucked in the harsh but sweet smoke. "Not wanting to show a light, eh?"

"You're pretty smart, ain't'cha? You're right. A match would shine across a dark prairie like a beacon in a lighthouse," he said, riding on.

"I'll give you this, marshal. You're tenacious. *Tenacious Marshal Mike Meagher, Marshal of Wichita.* How would you feel if I made that the title of a book I might write?"

"Puffed up."

"It's a darned good yarn, you know. One man riding off in pursuit of a pair of deadly desperadoes, tracking them through the dead of night, ready to shoot them on sight, thus saving the taxpayers the expense of a double hanging. That's exactly the thrilling stuff my publishers sent me out here for."

"First off, I ain't alone, am I? I got you beside me."

"Why did you let me come along? It sure wasn't because you figured you thought you'd need help. Must be a hundred men in town who'd be a lot more help than me."

"There wasn't exactly a throng of 'em demandin' to join the chase, was there? Fact is, you're the first man I ever met who cited a constitutional right to chance gettin' his head blowed off."

"Is that why you let me come?" said Tyrone, chuckling. "To have the pleasure of seeing a pain in the ass get his head blowed off?"

"The truth of it is, my friend, I didn't have the time to spare arguin' about it. Besides, I figured you'd drop out and head for town as soon as it got dark."

"Well, that's an honest answer."

"So what's kept you goin'? Pride? Or just plain Irish bullheadedness?"

"A little of both, I guess."

"That's honest."

"Mostly, though, it's the reporter in me. I never gave up on a story before and don't intend to start doing so now."

"The dictionary's got a word for that, you know!"

"Is that right?"

"Yeah," laughed Meagher. " 'Tenacious!' "

A few miles farther as they crested a low rise at full sunup, Meagher halted and pointed to the mound of a dwelling that was a half-mud, half-sod roof over a weathered wooden shack nestled on the still-shaded side of a hollow.

The faint whinny of a hungry horse drifted up the hill.

Tyrone whispered, "Do you think it's them?"

"Possibly. Then again, it could be anybody. A squatter, maybe. Or a traveler who chanced by and bedded down for the night."

Tyrone fingered the butt of his Colt. "So what do we do?"

Meagher scratched his chin thoughtfully. "We start by gettin' off these horses. Then we go belly-down in the grass and bide our time and see who comes out of that door to take a leak or tend the horse or . . . whatever."

The sheltering grass was sweet to the smell as Tyrone stretched out upon the hard, cool ground on the lip of the hollow. He realized how tired he was, aware of every sore muscle produced by a bumpy night in the saddle of a plodding horse that was now nibbling grass safely out of sight of the shack. Through his shirt, his aching back already felt the building heat of what was going to be another scorching day.

Then he smelled the fetchingly tantalizing aroma of cooking meat and perking coffee wafting up from the hollow on a breeze so slight it barely moved the grass.

"If it's them, they must be pretty sure of themselves to be riskin' a fire and smoke," whispered Meagher. "To do that they have to be damned confident they're not being tracked."

"Whatever it is that they're having for breakfast," sniffed Tyrone, "it smells mighty delicious. And the odor of that coffee's killing me, frankly!"

"Hold it," grunted Meagher, nodding toward the shack. "Look."

Below, a tall man moved from the shadow doorway into the light.

"That's Mickey," whispered Tyrone as Ludlum turned a corner of the shack.

A minute later, he returned, leading two horses.

"Good," sighed Meagher. "They're both down there."

At that moment, Moe stepped out, yawning and stretching.

"They don't seem to be in any rush, do they?" said Tyrone as the cousins stepped back into the shack. "They're gonna finish their breakfast, I suppose."

Meagher rose to a squat and pointed to the left. "You swing around and come down behind the shack on the shady side. Leave your hoss up here. Keep low in the grass. Don't want to spook those boys. I'll take the other side. Don't you do anything unless you have to. You leave everything to me. Got it?"

"You're the boss, marshal," said Tyrone, sliding forward snakelike in the sweet-smelling high grass, pausing only to wipe sweat from his face with a sleeve, to listen and to smell the aromas of the Ludlums' breakfast, a cruel reminder of how long it was since he'd had anything to eat. "Remember all these sensations," he said to himself. "Remember this for the book you're gonna write." If you survive, he thought grimly as he slid downward on his belly.

As he approached the rear of the shack it looked like nothing more than a large mound of earth but the smell of food was strong now and he could hear low voices inside. Creeping along the side of the shack, he drew his gun, crouched and waited.

A silence settled, as dead a quiet as he'd ever known.

The belly of the hollow baked in the rising heat and the shimmering air looked like simmering water in a pan as he searched the distant slope for any sign of a ripple in the grass that might be Meagher.

"C'mon, let's get a move on," said a voice in the shack—Mickey Ludlum barking impatiently.

"Jest hold your hosses. I ain't finished yet. You are the antsiest fella I ever did know," said Moe Ludlum.

"I'll stop bein' antsy onct we git to Mexico."

"I said it afore an' I'll say it agin. Don't know why you're in such a big hurry to git to Mexico. What the deuce is the rush? Ain't nobody after us. We got all the time in the world, so there's no call fer you to scurry me along when I ain't finished eatin' yet."

"Well when you do finish your grub I'll be outside."

The door creaked open.

Tyrone tensed.

The door banged shut.

Tyrone eased to his feet, pressing back against the rough planking of the shack's wall and hearing the soft scratch of a matchstick being struck.

A whiff of pungent tobacco smoke drifted around the corner.

Inside, boots clumped across the hard dirt floor moving toward the door.

Tyrone eased away from the wall and turned, raising his arms into a triangle with the Colt at the point. Cold sweat trickled down his sides. His mind screamed, "Where the hell's Meagher?"

"The hosses look tuckered out," said Moe. "Maybe we should rest 'em more."

"We rested them too damned long already as far as I'm concerned," growled Mickey. "That Wichita marshal could be right behind us."

"Y'know, brother," laughed Moe, "you always was the worry wart of the clan."

Jesus, where's Meagher, worried Tyrone.

The marshal of Wichita had never lost sight of him, shaking his head in half-disgust, half-amusement as Tyrone had made his sloppy way down to the shack. Head too high. Rump popping up now and then. The grass he was crawling through swaying as if it were caught in a cyclone. "Civilians," he'd muttered, spitting the word as if it were mud in his mouth. "Newspaper reporter! Freedom of the press! Ha!"

Yet in spite of everything, Tyrone had reached the shack unnoticed. Taking up a satisfactory backup position, he was perfectly placed in case the Ludlums tried to get away. That is, Meagher thought, if the kid wouldn't think it was ungentlemanly to shoot a man in the back.

He lifted his Winchester rifle and sighted on Mickey, the one who'd actually done the killing in the holdup of the drover.

He fired, drilling him in the middle of the chest.

Jerking in surprise, Moe ducked, just missing taking the second shot in the head.

For Tyrone, it was an instant stretched into lifetime. A pinpoint flash of red fire in yellow grass as brilliant as a firefly in black night. A bang, like the gun going off that had killed Crazy Sid. A thunking sound as the bullet hit. Mickey Ludlum letting out a puff of air, as if he'd been punched in the belly, then jerked backward like a puppet being yanked on a string, slamming against the wall.

A second muzzle flash was a long tongue of flame. A second bang seemed louder. Wood splintered as the bullet hit a wall.

"Missed," thought Tyrone, waiting for a third shot.

Suddenly, lurching around the corner, Moe Ludlum appeared with eyes wide open in surprise. "You!"

His right hand jerked instinctively toward his gun.

Tyrone fired.

Hit squarely in the middle of his belly, Moe spun backward, dropping hard, his boots kicking up a spray of dirt as he fell.

With time moving again, Tyrone eased forward, shaking, cold with sweat. Holding the Colt rigidly at the point of the triangle of his arms, he stepped from one body to the next, nudging each with the toe of his boot.

When he looked up, he saw the marshal sprinting across the hollow, his rifle slack at his side.

"Nice shooting," said Meagher, breathlessly, poking Moe Ludlum's boot with his own.

Tyrone's mouth was bone dry as he grunted. "I could hardly have missed."

The marshal studied Tyrone's pale face. "Are you feelin' all right?"

"For a fellow who's just shot somebody," said Tyrone, lifting his Stetson and wiping sweat from his forehead with the back of his hand, "I believe I feel fine."

"Well don't grieve for these boys," said Meagher coldly. "They were born bad and reared worse, so they were bound to die. Justice has been done."

TWELVE

The Curiosity

Looking like wax husks laid out in plain uncovered pine coffins that seemed a size too small for them, the Ludlums were propped up for display in the window of Melvin Granick's funeral parlor with their arms folded across their chests and hands clutching pistols.

No effort had been made to cover the bullet holes in their bloody shirts; indeed, they were the main attraction.

Crudely hand-printed on a cardboard pinned to Mickey's chest was:

MICHAEL "MICKEY" LUDLUM, SHOT BY MARSHAL MIKE MEAGHER

Attached to Moe was:

MOSES "MOE" LUDLUM, SHOT BY DEPUTY TYRONE

Spanning them at the knees was a sign that had been ordered by the town council and printed on Marsh Murdock's *Eagle* press:

WARNING

MURDERERS, THIEVES, FOOT-PADS

AND LOUNGERS
ARE NOT WELCOME IN WICHITA.

THIS WILL BE YOUR REWARD!

"Awful," Tyrone murmured as he stood with Marsh Murdock gazing at the sickening display. "Just plain awful. Pagan, even."

Curling an arm sympathetically around him, the editor teased. "I take it that this is not the custom back in civilized Little Old New York?"

"Hell no," said Tyrone, turning away. "It's disgusting."

"I never did believe in this sort of thing as a way of preventing crime," said Murdock, thoughtfully lighting a long black cigar. "I don't believe in public hangings either. I never knew one yet where some of the spectators didn't have their pockets picked while they watched." He lit the cigar. "But it's the way things are done in these parts," he went on, flipping the burnt match into the bone-dry street. "It's human nature," he said exhaling a plume of pungent smoke toward the Ludlums. "People are just plain curious." His eyes slid sidelong to Tyrone. "They're plenty curious about you, too, of course. The whole town's buzzing with your name. Probably the entire state!"

"That's just great," huffed Tyrone, jamming his hands into his hip pockets and walking away with a new twist to Morgan's unhappy Shakespearean phrase pounding inside his head—O God! Tyrone, what a wounded name! "What you're sayin' is that I can now expect every gunslick and owlhoot in Kansas to come riding into Wichita gunning for me?"

"You're big news, my friend," said the editor, falling into step beside him. "There's no getting around it." He touched Tyrone's shoulder gently, consolingly. "You have my personal sympathy. But . . . as you know, I run a newspaper, so I'm hoping you'll afford me a little of your time between now and my next edition so you can write up a personalized account of the event for the edification of the subscribers to the *Eagle.*"

Tyrone stopped short. "Hell no, Marsh!"

"A simple little interview!"

Tyrone walked on. "Get the facts from the marshal."

"Naturally I'll be talking to him. But it's not just the cold hard facts that I want. I want color! I need *your* angle—how you feel and so forth."

Tyrone winced. "The hell with that!"

"Whether you like it or not, *you* are the story, my friend," said Murdock urgently, pursuing him at run. "You're a hell of a lot better an angle than a routine account of a lawman doing his duty. You're a newspaperman yourself, so you know what I mean. Why, if you were in my shoes you'd be chasing the story yourself; the exciting account of how a stranger showed up in wild and woolly Wichita and out of a personal thirsting for righteousness and justice wound up deputized and ridding the town of the scourge of a pair of lawless ruffians who everybody agrees are better off dead. Now that is a beauty of a yarn. Every reporter's dream story!" He stopped short, his face twisted as if in pain. "Hey! You haven't by chance already telegraphed it back to Mr. Bennett in New York?"

Tyrone moaned and stomped his foot. "I told you I don't work for him anymore."

"Good," grinned Murdock, slapping Tyrone's back. "That means I'll have it exclusive! Maybe I'll peddle it to Bennett myself!" He laughed. "Wouldn't that be a hoot?"

"Yeah, it'd be a hoot all right," said Tyrone with a smile spreading across his face as his mind formed a tantalizing picture of Bennett reading about him. He barked a laugh. "The firm of Beadle and Adams might find it interesting, as well. Maybe they'd even demand I write my first book about myself!"

"Come to the office now," said Murdock excitedly, "and we'll get it all down on paper!"

"God, do you know what you are, Marsh? A buzzard!"
"It takes one to know one," cackled the editor.

The *Eagle* came out the next afternoon, the headlines stacked in the middle of the front page:

A DUEL TO THE DEATH
TYRONE'S OWN HEROIC STORY
How the Ludlums Reaped Their Just Reward!
"FAIR FIGHT," REPORTS MARSHAL MEAGHER:
The True Story in Tyrone's Words

Beneath stretched a double column of small gray print sprinkled with superlatives, each more unsettling than the previous. "What a load of manure," groaned Tyrone, crumpling the paper and flinging it across his hotel room. Rocketing from his chair, he thumped to the window and peered down at the swirl of Main Street, his racing imagination picking out the men who might be waiting for him to appear, their black hearts set on putting him to the test as gun-crazed glory-seekers must have stalked Morgan in his Abilene days.

Shouldn't've relented and given Marsh that interview, he thought. What to do? he wondered.

"The milk's spilled," he said bitterly. "Can't stay in this damned room forever."

He moved back from the window.

Plopping onto his bed, he caught his image in the mirror.

He stared, searching for any sign of change in him, for any outward sign of the raging contradiction he felt inside as he grappled with the sickening reality of killing Moe Ludlum with the glowing praise Marsh Murdock had put into his newspaper. "Hero?" he asked.

His eyes narrowed and through tight lips he muttered, "You're no hero. You're a damned fool, that's what you are."

His eyes drifted, falling on his gunbelt and holster curled like a black snake on a table, the butt of the pistol jutting out like a viper's head.

He remembered the feel of it in his hands, heavy and cold at the point of the triangle of his outstretched arms, as he faced Moe at the corner of the shack. It had been an instant, the wink of an eye, and in that split second Moe had moved. It had been little more than a flinch. Was Moe really going for his gun? Or had he simply been surprised? Would Moe have killed him? Might there have been a chance that Moe might have given up?

Rising from the bed, he crossed the room to the table where the gun lay.

Touched, the grip of the Colt was cool.

Suppose he hadn't fired?

What if he had waited a moment longer?

What if Moe had thrown up his arms and surrendered?

"He'd have been hanged," he said, easing the gun from the holster. "He was born to die."

Sliding the gun back, he picked up the gun belt.

"Fair fight," said the marshal to the editor in the *Eagle*. There'd been no choice as to what to do, he'd attested. "It was a case of Tyrone shooting to save his own life."

If any man doubted that, all he had to do was look in the window of Granick's funeral parlor and see the bullet hole in the front of Moe's shirt, the marshal told the editor.

But then Meagher said something that hit Tyrone with the force of a fist in the stomach.

"There's no question that Tyrone did the people of Kansas a service in ridding them of a pestilence, but I can only hope that in so doing he hasn't made himself a target for all the crazy gunmen who might get it into their twisted noggins that they can make a reputation for themselves by going up against Tyrone. Because of the chance it might happen, I'm exempting Tyrone from the ordinance against carrying firearms inside the town limits and naming Tyrone as a permanent deputy marshal."

Immediately on reading the words, Tyrone recalled Charlie Carew relating with relish what had happened to Morgan in Abilene after he'd killed the Dowd brothers. "Seemed like every gunslick for a hundred miles around showed up lookin' for Morgan! First was a scrawny kid named Foty, drawin' on Morgan in my saloon and dyin' in the effort. Next was a Texican called Francisco Raphael who called on Morgan to draw right in the middle of Texas Street, earnin' a spot in the cemetery."

Might something like that happen down there on Wichita's Main Street? Tyrone wondered as he gazed out at it. Might he hear his name called in the center of Douglas Street? Must he start to look at every face approaching him on the broad thoroughfare that cut through Delano as a potential threat? Would he have to adopt Mike Meagher's habit of always sitting with his back to the wall in Long Charlie's? From now on did he have to keep his eyes on the green batwing doors and measure every man who pushed through them as a danger?

"Hell, I can't stay in this room forever," he said angrily.

Putting on the gun belt, he turned toward the door.

But his reflection in the mirror held him.

He studied his face again.

Was there a change? A difference?

He'd come to Wichita in peace looking for someone whose story would thrill the readers of Beadle and Adams dime novels.

Now he was the one being written about in a newspaper.

He'd arrived in search of some tale to quench the curiosity of people who would never see the frontier themselves.

Now he was a curiosity.

His eyes slid down to the gun strapped to the hip of the image in the mirror.

As if it belonged to someone else, his hand rose from his side.

As if under a spell, he watched as the mirrored hand grasped the pistol, cleared it of the holster and came up level as though he were duelling with himself and, as if lightning were splitting him from head to toe, he felt a tingle surging through him, thrillingly.

THIRTEEN

Hot Streets

Sun-scorched July and the life of Alton Longley, age sixteen, went out with a bang. Shouting "Tyrone" as he appeared from an alley between Red Beard's Dance Hall and a saddlery, the cowboy from Austin had waited for Tyrone to turn before going for his Colt, but the gun was barely clear of the holster when Tyrone fired, spinning the boy like a top and back into the alley where he flopped like a fish for nearly a minute before dying.

The week after, a drunken Hector Cook took up a challenging but wobbly stance on the boardwalk in front of Long Charlie's. He collected a bullet to his right shoulder rather than a slug in the gut, as Tyrone instantly judged that it was the drink that had pushed him into a foolhardy act he never would have tried sober.

On a sultry Saturday evening in early August while standing at the bar in Long Charlie's, rather than be goaded into a gunfight by another cowboy not old enough to grow a respectable beard, he brained the kid with the long barrel of his Colt, a humiliation that sent the kid staggering out in tears, never to be seen in Wichita again.

"It's the heat as much as anythin' else that makes 'em do it," declared Carew.

It was a theory easy to accept. Since the day Tyrone had arrived, the summer had been a relentless oven, but the heat wave broke late in August, shattering amidst the boom and bang and lightning flashes of the wildest thunderstorms in Tyrone's experience. Rain that turned the broad streets of Wichita into mires of mud had the rivers running perilously close to flooding, halted the trains and mercifully ceased the commerce in cattle and visits to town by big-spending, thrill-starved cowboys who might get it into their heads to test their gunmanship against the hotshot duelist everybody'd heard about.

"Cussed weather," groaned Charlie Carew as he leaned behind his nearly unpopulated bar on the fourth night of relentless downpours.

"A few days ago you were down on the weather on account of the heat," retorted Tyrone as his attention drifted to the rear of the room and a small cluster of stranded livestock traders gathered around the dart board.

Toeing the throwing line and squinting at the board down the shaft of a dart stood a giant of a man—six feet five, Tyrone estimated, and probably in his forties—with buckskin trousers tucked into gleaming knee-high brown boots, a pale yellow silk shirt worn with the collar open and showing chest hair as thick as a bearskin and a bull-like neck encircled by a crimson kerchief beneath a full beard.

A blackboard with the scoring chalked upon it indicated that the giant needed 80 points to win.

His opponent, a middle-aged, beer-bellied redhead, looked worried.

The giant threw, hitting the bullseye for 50, leaving him needing only 30 to win, which he achieved with a double 15.

"Good arrows, Shang," praised the defeated redhead.

The giant turned to search the room with narrowed, challenging eyes. "Who's next?"

"Who wants to be slaughtered?" muttered the vanquished redhead.

"I'll give it a try," declared Charlie Carew, lurching from behind the bar.

When he tossed his first dart, it was almost casually, giving the impression he could have made the point blindfolded. "Twenty," announced the redhead as he chalked Carew's score on the board.

"Go for double tops, Charlie," shouted Tyrone.

Instantly, the giant spun around, glaring at him. "No coaching, please!"

Carew's dart slammed into the 20 at the top of the board.

"Well, well, well, Shang," chided the redhead as he marked the score, "looks like you are about to be canned."

"It ain't over till it's over," grumbled the giant, throwing a winning treble twenty. Coming up straight with his massive throwing hand closing into a fist, he turned and yelled at Tyrone. "How's that, stranger?"

Tyrone strode toward him. "Congratulations, sir."

"Would you care for a game, young man?"

"Ah, I'm not very good at it."

The giant squinted. "The hell you ain't."

"I'm out of your league, I assure you, Mr., uh . . ."

"Able Head Pierce is my name, but known all over as Shanghai."

"I'm Tyrone."

"Ah, yes! The New York Irishman who helped put the Ludlum boys out of business! You're quite the topic of conversation around here. A hero!"

"That's mighty kind of you to say, Mr. Pierce, but . . ."

"Shanghai! Everybody calls me Shanghai. Or Old Shang. Or just plain Shang."

Recovering from his defeat by drawing himself a mug of warm beer, Carew spoke up. "Tyrone's here to write a book, Shang."

"It's an author you are then? Have I read one of your tomes? I'm very big on the readin' of hist'ry. Now take the game of darts. It's got quite a story! Just as the pastime is a relief from boredom for these cowboys, darts broke the boredom of soldiers between battles long-since forgotten. Far from women and left to their own entertainments, they'd idly compete by shooting arrows into the bottoms of wine casks, then progressed to the round slices of downed trees that provided natural concentric rings for the purpose of determining points. As the target aged and cracked, radial lines became further delineation of scoring. With the coming of winter, the boards were moved indoors by the hearth fire, requiring a modification of the implements being aimed at the target and, thus, the invention of a shortened and hand-thrown arrow—the dart itself. Indoor rules were devised. Better boards were fashioned. Soon the cold and drafty castles in all parts of the British Isles were scenes of rousing and raucous games and tournaments. Kings took them up and it was said that Ann Boleyn gave a set of darts to Henry VIII, although there was considerable doubt about the claim that it was because she beat him at the game that caused him to have her beheaded. Always a manly pursuit, refined over the centuries from its rudimentary beginnings and carried to the corners of the world as Britain built its empire, darts became a sport associated with the pubs of England. Now they are found in drinking establishments everywhere! Despite your assertion that you're not very good at the game, I'd wager that you threw your share of darts back in New York City!"

"I tossed from time to time," smiled Tyrone, shying away from admitting that those who'd competed with him in the Garden of Eden, including McGlory himself, had judged him excellent.

"Tyrone's got his heart set on writin' about cowboys," interjected Carew, "but I'm tryin' to convince him that it's me he should write about."

"Who the hell wants to read a short book about a tall man," scoffed Pierce. "So what about you and I havin' that game of darts, Tyrone?"

"If you want to sully your reputation by playing with an amateur, darts it is," Tyrone said.

Effortlessly, he hit a treble 20 with his first dart, the same with his second and the bull for 50 on the third, giving him a score of 170.

"Good darts, Tyrone," crowed Carew. "Looks like I finally found somebody who can beat this old Texas fart at his own game."

"Hush," snapped Tyrone, jabbing Carew in the ribs with an elbow and nodding at Pierce. "Can't you see the man's trying to concentrate?"

"Kibbitzing never rattles me," grunted Shanghai. "In fact, it helps."

After opening with a treble 20, he aimed to repeat Tyrone's throws but came up with a treble 19 and then the bull for 167, a three-point deficit that dogged his game to the end when he needed 63. This required a treble 11 and double 15 while Tyrone needed 60—an easy goal for a player as handy at hitting 20s as Tyrone seemed to be, thought Pierce. Throwing treble 11 was easy but the final dart hit the wire to the right of the double 15 and landed in double 10, finishing him. "Nice throwin'," he said after Tyrone collected his 20s to win. "We had no wager, but since you beat me, I'll buy the whiskey. But first I have to go out back and see a man about a horse."

"It's wet enough without you pissin'," cackled Carew.

Bellying up to the bar, Tyrone asked, "What's his story, Charlie?"

"I hope you ain't figurin' on writin' about him."

"Can't say till I know more. He seems interesting. How well do you know him?"

"Pretty well. He was born in Rhode Island. Spent some time at sea. Now he's one of the biggest names in the Texas cattle trade. One of the founders of the market here in Wichita. He went from a handful of mavericks at the start to over fifteen thousand head branded last season on the spread he calls Rancho Grande in Matagorda."

"How's a Texan who was transplanted from New England wind up with the monicker Shanghai?"

"There's different versions as to that. The first is that he was snatched off a Boston wharf—shanghai'd onto a merchant ship that was undermanned. Another is that he suddenly appeared one day in Shanghai beggin' to be hired by the captain of a New England-bound ship, tellin' a story of bein' the orphaned son of missionaries who'd died and left him stranded. At various times, Shang has told each of those yarns and sworn to them. The third account is that he got the nickname to distinguish him from another man named Pierce, but of lesser stature and shorter legs. The fourth theory holds that somebody looked at him one night in a cantina in San Antonio and got an eyeful of Pierce struttin' around wearin' spurs with rowels the size of windmills and remarked that he looked like a Shanghai rooster. Not everybody shares my admiration for him. That's jealousy, mostly."

"What are they jealous about?"

"A man who's bigger than most in more ways than physically is apt to rub lesser men the wrong way. Some claim that he's less than square, but he's never wronged me."

"Where's Matagorda?"

"That's an island down in Texas. San Antonio Bay is on one side and the Gulf of Mexico on the other. Shanghai calls his spread El Rancho Grande—the Big Ranch. They say it's the biggest ranch of all."

"There's no doubt about it," thundered Pierce, returning to the bar. "A million acres, at least, but who's countin'?" Throwing a heavy arm across Tyrone's shoulders, he bellowed, "So you're the fellow who plugged Moe Ludlum! That's a deed that calls for a celebration. You name what you're drinkin', son. And put away your money! Shanghai Pierce will be doin' the payin'."

"Bein' a son of the auld sod, the man only imbibes Irish," exclaimed Carew, bringing the bottle.

"You seem pleased over the demise of the Ludlums, Mr. Pierce," said Tyrone.

"Call me Shanghai, son, and, yes, I am pleased. Those hooligans had the temerity to rob and kill an honest cattleman. Had they not been promptly punished, the affair would have been bad for business. I'm a businessman. And I make it my business to foster business. That's why I salute you, young man. You did the cattle business of Wichita, indeed, the cattle business everywhere, a distinct service when you shot down that scurvy thug."

"Actually, Shanghai, the cattle business had nothing to do with it. It was either him or me and besides . . ."

"A mere technicality," Shanghai boomed, slapping Tyrone's back.

"I was going to say," Tyrone continued, "that the credit for bringing the Ludlums to justice belongs to Marshal Meagher."

"Oh, he's a fine lawman! In praisin' you I do not detract a whit from the credit due to the marshal. I'd be the last to question his stellar record in maintaining law and order in Wichita. In fact, I had the pleasure of recommending him to the founding fathers of this fair city. And he's done a splendid job, eh, Charlie?"

"First rate," said Carew, topping their glasses.

"And as honest as the day is long," said Shanghai. "Not all men who wear a badge are," he added.

"Hear, hear," said Carew, pounding the bar.

"Tell me more about this book you're writin'."

"Truth is, I haven't written a word!"

"How long will you be stayin' in Wichita?"

"All summer observing the breed, I suppose. Then I'll probably spend the winter doing the writing."

"Kansas is fine in summertime but no place to be in the winter. You'll freeze your ass off, believe me! You should come down to Texas. Come visit with me. You'll have the peace and quiet of El Rancho Grande and since you're interested in the true story of the cowboys, it's just the place for you to see 'em up close where they live. Yes, I believe it's the perfect spot for you to do your writin'. And I'd enjoy your comp'ny."

"That's generous, Shanghai. I'll mull it over!"

FOURTEEN

Down to Texas

September, and Wichita was slowing down. Days were cooler and shorter and the nights were getting long. Save for a few straggling herds, the season of the cattle drives was over. Though disappointed, Charlie Carew was not surprised when Tyrone declared that he was taking up Shanghai Pierce's invitation to winter in Texas.

To show him the way, he hired a pair of brothers, the last of the cowboys who'd arrived in July from the Hebert ranch a little south of San Antonio.

Jeb Slade was the older—long and lanky, dark and quiet, smart.

Roy was fair-haired, with a quick smile as bright as the sun, but slow.

Their reason for taking Tyrone with them was the money he offered them, their own funds having been spent, as Roy described it, "sportin' in Wichita."

At first they were amused to see him hunching over and scribbling in his notebooks each night beside their campfire, ribbing him and riding him about it, but soon they were asking him to read his words to them and demanding to be shown their names on the pages if he had written about them that day. Then they became contributors, pointing out incidents which they believed worthy of his journal and telling him things he didn't know—the name of a kind of tree, what a place was called, a landmark and why it was important, the names of the creeks, streams and rivers they crossed—the Arkansas, Cimarron and Canadian, so far. There would be more to cross in Texas, they told him, starting with the Red. Then would come the Trinity, the Colorado, the Brazos and the Guadelupe before they reached the San Antonio. At that point they would turn west toward home and Tyrone would proceed east to El Rancho Grande on the coast.

The Red River was running high when they came to it late on the 15th of September and decided to camp until morning.

"More than three hundred miles from Wichita," he noted in his journal. "More than that to go."

The land he was entering, his companions proceeded to tell him as if they had a single voice, was vast and largely untamed. There were mountains and plateaus in the west—a brutal space known in Spanish as *Llano Estacado,* called the Staked Plains in English, though they couldn't tell him why. In the east he would find a long stretch of marshlands and if he went far enough he'd encounter sandy beaches washed by the waters of the Gulf of Mexico. "That's where Matagorda is," said Roy.

They promised him sprawling forests of blackjack oak and loblolly pines, millions of acres of rolling prairies, hills and lush valleys teeming with wildlife.

And far to the south between the rivers San Antonio and Nueces was the longhorn cattle country known as the Nueces Strip.

Goliad, the location of the Colter Ranch, they told him when he asked about Morgan, was in the heart of it. "Texas, here I come," he laughed as he coaxed Redskin into the surging Red River that was a cold kiss as it enveloped them.

The next would be the Trinity, seventy miles due south, and the town where they'd be crossing was named Fort Worth.

In midafternoon, at a distance, they observed a small herd of cattle lumbering northward. "They're movin' late in the season," asserted Jeb.

Tyrone watched them through a shimmering haze, lifting his sweat-ringed hat to block out the sun as the cattle spilled across the rim of a low hill like a spreading brown stain on the parched grass.

He watched until there was nothing more to see, then turned his head and gently booted Redskin in the expectation of fording the Trinity by noon and having lunch, dinner and a night's sleep in a hotel at Fort Worth.

From there the route the Slade brothers chose was straight south.

On the third day they crossed the Brazos on the ferry at Waco but bypassing the noise and bustle of the town and pressing on to set up a camp at twilight beside an oak-lined creek of clear cold water and lush with jackrabbit. The next night they laid out blankets and saddles for beds in soft grass under a star-studded black sky beside a pretty creek teeming with fish that were so fat and lazy that they were able to scoop them up with hats. The following evening they camped alongside a wide and swift river named by the cowboys as the Colorado. Deer were rampant and supper was roasted venison.

The next day they were at the San Antonio. "This is where we part comp'ny," said Jeb. "Unless you'd care to change your mind and come along with us to San Antone."

"Thanks," Tyrone replied, stroking Redskin's neck, "but I'm bound for Matagorda, if you'll be kind enough to shove me in the proper direction."

"Just follow this river till you're hip deep in the ocean," grinned Roy. "You can't miss it!"

By dusk on the next day of riding alone, when the air

suddenly turned chilly and moist and the wind from the east tasted of salt, he knew he was near the sea. Booting Redskin into a trot, he felt excitement building. Then he was looking up at seagulls wheeling in graceful circles against the purple sky, their shrieks shattering the silence. At nightfall he made camp and stretched out on his bedroll beside a fire built of brush and drifted to sleep, lulled by the sigh of the cool, wet, salty ocean breeze.

Gulls doing sky cartwheels awoke him in a yellow daybreak.

At mid-morning, Redskin waded the shallow water between the mainland and the flats of Matagorda Island, a great sand bar stretching as far as he could see on each side.

Following fresh horse tracks in the sandy earth, he turned north until, an hour later, he halted Redskin, hooked a leg on the saddle horn and peered across a prairie of bearded salt rye at the slash of brilliant color that was the Mexican tile rooftop of a rambling house with whitewashed adobe walls and orange-tiled roof that rested like a crown on the highest rise of land for miles around.

"I see you found my humble abode," thundered Shanghai Pierce as Tyrone rode up to the house. With buckskin trousers tucked into gleaming knee-high brown boots, a pale yellow silk shirt worn with the collar open and his bullish neck encircled by a crimson kerchief, he was standing at the edge of a terrace with the sun-flaked blue-green waters of the Gulf of Mexico behind him. "You're just in time for supper. Hope you have a taste for wild boar!"

"Since I came out west," chucked Tyrone, "I seem to have developed a taste for anything that's new. And there's nothing I could see that'd surprise me!"

His bedroom had a plain, free-standing mirror that riveted his attention and what he found in its glass was not the same person who'd surveyed himself nearly a year ago in a whorehouse mirror in New York City, nor in the mirror in his room at the Harris House in Wichita. He'd been a boy then, he realized, but staring back at him now was the man he'd thought he was back then—no taller, save for the lift of his boot heels, but a lot wiser, tougher and harder.

Slung low from his hip and tied with a rawhide thong to his slender thigh hung the worn leather holster Morgan had picked out for him and in it the revolver that killed Moe Ludlum, the event which more than any other had turned that green boy into this brazen man.

At that moment, he decided that it was the figure in the mirror he had to write about. He was going to be the hero of the book! The others he'd met—Morgan, Mike Meagher, Charlie Carew, Dalgo, the salesman on the train, the drover gunned down and robbed on Main Street and the Ludlums—would be the characters who'd honed a raw kid from the streets of New York into a man capable of killing one of the worst owlhoots in Kansas. And he knew exactly how it would begin:

> When a pair of hardcases known as the Ludlum Boys barged through the green batwing doors of Long Charlie Carew's saloon on a sultry August night in Wichita, the steely-eyed cousins were not looking for a pair of cold beers to wet their whistles.
>
> Every man in the smoke-filled saloon knew they'd come there gunning for a new kid in town known as Irish.

Part Two:

THE BOOK OF KNAVES

FIFTEEN

The Book of Knaves

Warmed by the breezes off the Gulf of Mexico, the weeks passed quickly, marked by awakenings to golden dawns and chatty breakfasts with Shanghai on the veranda, mornings hunting the wild boars called javelinas, azure afternoons left alone with his writing, boisterous suppers savored on the west-facing porch drenched in golden sunsets and cool evenings in quiet, thoughtful conversation with the lord of El Rancho Grande. In the last week of December, he proudly announced to Shanghai that the work on the book was completed.

Reading it in one night while Tyrone roamed anxiously through the house, Shanghai pronounced it fine, hugging Tyrone and declaring, "I am mighty proud that it was written in my house."

Two days later, tightly wrapped in heavy brown paper, *Showdown in Hell Town* was on its way to Beadle and Adams of New York by way of the weekly mail hack to Houston.

Christmas came and with it lively celebrations as Shanghai Pierce played host to friends and neighbors. For a week every room of his Casa Blanca was filled. They congregated for drinks on the terrace at dusk and brought animated conversation to a crowded dinner table, much of it centered on Tyrone and his book whose hero was called Irish and bore a strong resemblance to the author.

As the year waned, the last of the visitors to El Rancho Grande was the freshly-elected Governor of Texas.

The Honorable Richard Coke appeared to Tyrone to be every inch the politician, but beneath a gentlemanly veneer of fine clothing and excellent speech Tyrone detected flint.

Accompanying the governor was a Texas Ranger, Lieutenant Andy Wofford.

More than six feet tall, broad-shouldered and sun-bronzed, his clothing suited him—a weathered ten gallon hat, homespun shirt, buckskin jacket and corduroy pants tucked into black boots cut straight across the tops. The character underneath this rough exterior, Tyrone judged, was as steeled as the Colt pistol he carried low-slung on his right hip from a black cartridge belt studded with ammunition. At the other hip dangled an Indian-bead sheath holding a bone-handled Bowie knife.

Dressed in a crisp white linen suit, a blue cotton shirt, crimson neckerchief and wearing white snakeskin boots, Shanghai poured wine the shade of a rose into tall crystal glasses with delicate stems as servants brought the first course of huge, steaming pink shrimp. "There's nothing that whets the appetite like the fruits of the sea," he gushed. "And how rife is the land around here with succulent food! Of course, there's beef! But the landscape teems with wild boar. And you don't have to go far to bag a heap of quail, turkey and every other sort of game bird. The place is a veritable Eden, eh, Governor?"

"The day is coming when all of Texas will be a garden of delights," replied Coke, spearing a shrimp with a fork. "I promise you that the day is not long off when Texas will be made safe for decent citizens from the Rio Grande to the Red River, from the Gulf waters to the Pecos."

"Now, now, Richard, you've already been elected," chided Shanghai, "so please spare us your tree-stump oratory."

For three hours they ate off silver plates with silver utensils and washed down each course with a different wine served in glittering crystal. Cigars and brandy were offered in the parlor, a vaulting chapel-like space with rich wood-paneled walls festooned with the trophies of Shanghai's hunts and lined with glass-fronted gun cases. "That's quite an arsenal you've got there, Shanghai," declared Lieutenant Wofford admiringly.

"Indeed so," beamed Shanghai, opening one of the cases and taking down a rifle. "And here's my newest! This is one of the first of the new Winchesters, Model '73."

"Mighty pretty," said Wofford as Shanghai passed it to him.

"The magazine's got a capacity of fifteen rounds," said Shanghai. Wofford raised the rifle and sighted a boar's head trophy on the wall. "Fires a .44-40 round."

"It's a dandy," sighed Wofford, returning the gun to the rack.

The conversation turned to politics, dominated by the governor, but it wasn't until the talk turned to the purpose of their journey to San Antonio that Tyrone paid more than scant attention, his ears perking up as the governor launched a tirade against rampant lawlessness along the Rio Grande. "I've decided to clean up that mess," he asserted, jabbing the air with a smoldering cheroot. "I'm unleashing the Texas Rangers. That's why I'm passing through your territory, Shanghai. There's to be a meeting on the subject in San Antonio on Tuesday. The Rangers are going to lay out a plan to start rooting out these scum once and for all."

"I'm damned glad to hear it, Richard," thundered Shanghai.

"It was a promise I made when I ran for governor and I assure you it wasn't just a lot of hot air on my part. The time's long past for the state government to rely either on the army or the citizens themselves to handle the problem. I don't blame the residents. It's been the history of these border counties that when any man, Mexican or American, has made himself prominent in hunting these lawless creatures down, or in organizing parties to go after them, he has been forced to move off his land or has been killed. You'll recall that Buck Colter was killed not long ago in a raid on the Flores gang at Las Cuevas."

"Texas lost one of its greatest men that day," replied Shanghai, "and I lost a dear friend."

"We owe it to him and all the peaceable people of the border country to put an end to these no-account trouble-makers," said the governor, chopping the air with his cigar for punctuation.

Shanghai peered across the smoky room at a clock atop the mantel. "Look at the time," he bellowed. "We'll want to be up early if we're going to make it to San Antone by Tuesday."

"You're coming along, then?"

"Wouldn't miss it," bellowed Shanghai.

When Tyrone awoke, it was with the first faint glow of dawn but rather than lie in bed waiting for the others to rouse themselves, he dressed and stepped out into the lemon light of the veranda. He gazed wonderingly at the broad stretch of the gray Gulf of Mexico stretching in the distance, then turned his back on the view to gaze up at the whitened walls of Shanghai Pierce's Casa Blanca set like a jewel in the heart of his Rancho Grande. Going inside, he passed through his bedroom into the hallway, quietly passing the heavy oaken door of his host's room and those of the other guests, wandering to the parlor with its racks filled with firearms.

Examining the gleaming new Winchester, he was startled by a voice. "You're an early riser, too, I see."

"Good morning, Lieutenant Wofford," said Tyrone, turning abruptly.

"That truly is a handsome weapon," said the Ranger longingly, nodding at the rifle. "I wish my outfit had a hundred like it. The Rangers could use a few more good guns . . . and men, especially now that the governor's ordered us to . . . well, you heard him last night!"

"Yeah, that was some speech."

"He meant every word of it, believe me. Yes, in him Texas at last has a law and order man. He's all for the Rangers."

Tyrone grinned. "And you're all for anyone who's all for the Rangers!"

"What I'm for is Texas. And right now, as the governor said, the future of Texas lies in the hands of the Rangers!"

With mounting enthusiasm, he explained the conditions which had preceded the election of Richard Coke. After the war, lawlessness had flourished while law enforcement hit a new low, he said darkly. Texas was rocked by scandal and corruption! A feeble attempt at setting up a state police force in 1870 had been scuttled by the politicians. "It was nothing but political hacks and pay-offs," he spat bitterly. "Scalawags and carpetbaggers! Succeeding E.M. Pease as governor in 1869, Edmund J. Davis had had on his hands a force that was nothing but an infernal engine of oppression," he declared. "The people were pretty fed up with being under the feet of buffalo soldiers, so they booted Davis out last year, picking Mr. Coke as governor. Things have been looking up ever since, starting with putting Major Johnny Jones in charge of organizing the Frontier Battalion."

"That's your outfit?" asked Tyrone.

"I'm proud to say it is! We're six companies of seventy-five men each, responsible only to Major Jones and

Governor Coke. My immediate superior officer is Captain Lee McNelly. Our territory is the Mexican border with authority to cross the Rio Grande to clean out the nests of these vipers and scoundrels. That's a privilege that even the United States Army had been denied." He paused to pull a gray paper-covered book from the pocket of his buckskin jacket. "They're all listed in here," he said, waving the book. "We call it the Book of Knaves. Listed in those pages are the names, aliases and descriptions of about three thousand of the worst scoundrels in Texas. Each is wanted for some crime or other ranging from murder to cattle thieving." Leafing through it, he stopped at the names listed under the letter S. "Here's the one we want most," he said, passing the book to Tyrone and tapping a finger on the page. "He's got a gang that holes up at a godforsaken spot he calls Hezekiah. It's in the hill country on the west bank of the Nueces, past Uvalde. We know its general location but never have been able to find it exactly. Of all the knaves in this little book, this is the one Captain McNelly's set his sights on."

Tyrone read:

SALDANA, Refugio Gonzales Ruis. Wanted for murder, kidnapping, robbery, cattle rustling. Warrants: Texas, New Mexico, Arizona.

Description: age, 30; 6'6", 230 lbs., brown hair, brown eyes, reddish skin, scar on right cheek, gold front tooth with inset diamond.

Background: born in Mexico, associated with the Cortinistas until age 15 when he fled to Taos, New Mexico to avoid prosecution for murder; subsequently, moved to live with a cousin, Sostenes, in Tascosa, Texas; at age 17, drifted to Eagle Pass region where he became associated with John King Fisher; operates hideaway called Hezekiah, vicinity of Uvalde.

Tyrone slapped the book into Wofford's palm. "That sure is a lot of lawlessness to be attributed to one man."

"That cousin, Sostenes, is just as bad. If we could wipe

them both out we'd send a clear message to all the others in this book that they're no longer safe," said Wofford, slipping the book into his pocket. "And we will get them!" He picked up the Winchester and fondled it admiringly. "Yes sir, it's a mighty fine rifle. It's well above what Rangers are issued." He replaced the Winchester in the gun rack lovingly and inspected the other guns until he found the one he was looking for. "The Sharps rifle," he said, taking down the gun and sounding like a school teacher addressing a class of students. "They call these 'Beecher's Bibles' in memory of the Reverend Henry Ward Beecher. The good reverend was not exactly against applying gunpowder in advancing a just and holy cause. Neither are you, I'm told." He put the gun back tenderly then turned, grinning. "Shanghai told me how you gunned down Moe Ludlum up in Kansas."

"If you're trying to recruit me into the Rangers, I can only say that I'm flattered, but I'm a writer, not a gunman."

"Oh, you got me wrong," blurted Wofford. "I wasn't trying to enlist you. I was just supposin' that the Texas Rangers going after one of the hardest cases in the West might make a pretty good story. As to you being a Ranger yourself, well, the main ingredient of a Ranger is strength of character, and I'd say you've already demonstrated that you have plenty of it."

"That's very kind of you to say it."

"It's the truth. It's obvious you've got grit. You and Captain McNelly would hit it off, I'm sure. As a writer who's looking for subjects, you ought to meet him. And, like they say, there's no time like the present! Or is there something more important to hold you here?"

"A week ago there would have been. I was working on my book. But that's finished and on its way back East."

Wofford beamed. "So there's nothin' to keep you from ridin' over to San Antone? Great!"

"Well, I will be needing a subject for my next book.

Who knows? It could turn out to be you," said Tyrone, teasingly.

"Me?" gasped Wofford. "Thunderation, all you could write about me wouldn't take up half a page! McNelly's the one you should write about! He's a genuine get down and get to it man's man, the very backbone of the Rangers. Believe me, now that he's been put in charge of cleanin' the west country, thing's are gonna happen real fast. Why, he . . ."

Like a clap of thunder, the voice of Shanghai Pierce silenced him. "Thought I heard voices!" Dressed for riding, he loomed in the doorway. "Mornin', gentlemen. You're up and at 'em mighty early. Beds too soft? Too hard? Last night's meal didn't upset your digestions, I hope?"

"On the contrary," said Wofford.

"You're eager to get goin', I expect," said Shanghai. "I can tell that you're a man who's most at home with a saddle for a pillow and chores to be done." His glance turned to Tyrone. "And do I detect the gleam of adventure in those Irish eyes of yours, my friend?"

"Tyrone's comin' along to San Antone to meet Captain McNelly," answered Wofford.

"Is he to be the subject of your next book?" asked Shanghai.

"Andy's mighty high on him," said Tyrone lightheartedly, "so I figured I'd better investigate."

"I take that as a tribute to McNelly," replied Shanghai, crossing the room to a box of cigars on his massive desk. "The measure of a leader is the esteem in which he's held by those who serve under him. The true leader is the one who sets an example." He paused to offer them cigars and to light them. "Give me the man who's leading the charge! The general at the fore of his troops! The laurels belong to the man in the fray, whose face is marked by the dust and sweat and blood of the battle. Give me a man who strives valiantly and spends himself in a worthy cause.

That sort of man, even if he fails, is a great man who will tower over timid souls who know neither victory nor defeat."

"Well said, sir," exclaimed Wofford.

"Such a man, in my estimation, is General Porfirio Diaz," said Shanghai, leading them to the veranda, already alight with the rising sun. "Now, I appreciate that there are some Texans who take a dim view of Diaz, seeing him as a troublesome Mexican upstart who'll make trouble for Texas. But I see him as the only hope for an eventual settlement of the troubles along the border. There's a man also worthy of your pen, Tyrone!"

"Excuse my ignorance," answered Tyrone, "but I never heard of him."

"Jose de la Cruz Porfirio Diaz, a mestizo," said Shanghai, settling into a cane chair facing the sea and rising sun. "He came to my attention when he supported Juarez against the French and their puppet dictator, Maximilian, and then lost to Juarez in the presidential election in '71. He's been leading a revolt against the government ever since. I expect—I hope—that one day he'll win, for only then will we who live next door to Mexico be able to work out a settlement of our difficulties. That includes the extermination of the lawless element that currently vexes Lieutenant Wofford and his Rangers and is to be the subject of this meeting being convened by Governor Coke in San Antonio. I'm glad you've elected to come with us, Tyrone. It should be an education."

SIXTEEN

The Nueces Strip

They split up at Refugio with the governor and Shanghai proceeding together toward San Antonio while Tyrone and Wofford cut north toward Goliad and the Colter Ranch. It was Shanghai's idea. "I don't expect Morgan to join us now that he and Rebecca have got a new baby," he explained, "but the two of 'em should be apprised of what's happenin'. The Colter ranch has suffered as much as any in the territory. Andy, you can fill Morgan in on the particulars. And you, Tyrone, you prob'ly would like to renew your acquaintanceship with him?"

"It's hardscrabble country," said Wofford as their horses waded through the brush on the south bank of the Blanco River, running low as they crossed to the north. A cluster of cottonwoods cast a circle of enticing shade that looked perfect for resting themselves and their horses. They aimed to reach Goliad and the Colter ranch before sundown.

Picking up a stick, Wofford drew a wiggling line in the dirt. "This is the Nueces River," he explained. "Some call it the Sheriff's Deadline because south of it is nothin' but lawlessness. It's cattle country, of course. Longhorn territory. Bandit country. A rustler's heaven!"

He drew a second line six inches from the first.

"This here's the Rio Grande."

Scribbling between the two rivers, he said, "The triangle of land betwixt it and the Nueces is called the Nueces Strip, three hundred miles long and a hundred miles wide. The part on both sides of the Rio Grande's also been called Zona Libre, or Free Zone. It's been the stomping grounds of Mexican bandits known as the Cortinistas, after their boss, a hardcase named Juan Nepomuceno Cortina and also called the Red Robber of the Rio Grande, on account of his reddish skin. He's one of the worst cutthroats ever to ride a hoss. Just as bad as him was Cortina's right-hand man, Saldana, who's got the blessing of Cortina to run his own gang, as long as Cortina gets a cut of the action."

"I can see you've got your work cut out for you," said Tyrone, munching a strand of dried beef.

"There's a third player in this rotten game, another bad apple, name of John Fisher, known in the Strip as the King," said Wofford. "He's got a ranch on the Pendencia Creek near Eagle Pass." He tapped the stick on the high end of the line marking the Rio Grande. "In fact, the whole region around Eagle Pass has come to be called King Fisher's Territory. He does a good deal of illegal business with the Cortinistas and he and Saldana are very tight, but so far we haven't been able to get the evidence to pin any criminal charges on Fisher."

He tossed the stick into the river, angrily.

"We will get him, too, eventually," he said emphatically. "But because we don't have the manpower at this time to go over into Mexico to grab the Cortina gang, right now it's Saldana that we're concentratin' on."

He stood and dusted the seat of his pants. "Findin' his exact hidin' place is our problem. He's got a hole in the high ground, called Hezekiah, northwest of Uvalde. It's not on any map and those who know where it lies are, as you might imagine, reluctant to talk." He studied the cloudless sky. "I reckon we should hit Morgan's place in time for supper."

Before the war, Goliad had been a sunbaked way station along an old cart trail winding its way up from Mexico. But since the conflict ended it had grown to be a thriving and bustling crossroads as new settlers arrived, travelers paused en route farther west and the livestock business flourished, thanks to the opening of cattle trails that led to the new railroads in the new towns of Kansas.

Among the earliest settlers had been Arbuckle Colter. Born in 1800 on a small farm on the Louisiana side of the Mississippi, he'd been raised by his French-born father to believe that the destiny of the United States of America was to build a nation that would span the continent from ocean to ocean. Consequently, this passionate belief led him to enlist in an expedition of adventuresome Louisianans who marched into Texas in 1821 to capture a Mexican fort at Goliad and to fashion the area safe for settlement by Americans. In 1835, with the Texas Revolution only seven days old, he joined an armed force in driving out a Mexican garrison and had signed a declaration of independence for Texas. The following March, he was one of more than 300 Texas soldiers massacred by Santa Anna's troops, dying with a bullet fired into the back of his head as he was forced to kneel inside the Mission Nuestra Senora del Espiritu Santo de Zuniga.

In addition to this public history, a family memory of the patriarch of the Colters of Goliad was abundantly evident within the sturdy adobe walls of the house he had built on the bluffs overlooking the San Antonio River and which had been greatly expanded by his heirs.

Upon the death of the patriarch, the ranch had been

inherited by his 22-year-old son. A youth with a natural genius for the livestock business and an appreciation for real estate, David Colter soon extended the ranch from the southern banks of the San Antonio River to encompass a hundred thousand acres of legally owned land and upwards of one million acres which he deemed to be rightfully his simply because his cattle grazed upon them, reaching as much as 60 miles south and west.

There was no telling how much more of the Nueces Strip he might have claimed had he not been shot to death in 1862, thus bequeathing everything to his son, the second Arbuckle. Reared to the business of stock ranching, Buck had been put in charge of his first northern cattle drive in 1857 at the age of 23, crossing the Missouri near Independence and selling the herd in Illinois, for twenty-five dollars a head paid in gold.

One of those coins mounted on a slab of oak he kept on his huge walnut desk in a light and breezy room with walls decorated with hunting trophies in the west wing of what had become since his grandfather's day a rambling ranch house with thick adobe walls and a roof of rounded orange Mexican tiles. It meandered like a river from the original two room house to a dozen rooms in four wings around a Spanish-style courtyard that commanded a view that encompassed Colter property all the way to the southwestern horizon and far beyond.

A centerpiece of the parlor of the house was a lifesize oil painting of the founder of the empire displayed above the hearth. Flanking it in heavy wooden cases were the journals he'd kept beginning on the day he'd pulled up stakes in Louisiana. Bound in brick-red morocco leather by his grandson, Arbuckle Colter the Second, the volumes overflowed with the pioneer's keen insights into the empressarios, heroes and worldly saints who laid the foundations of Texas.

Because Buck Colter had been killed in a battle with

cattle thieves at Las Cuevas, Mexico, the ranch now belonged to his beautiful daughter Rebecca.

Wearing a buckskin vest over a plain blue cotton shirt, brown riding pants and knee-high black boots as she sat in an armchair before the portrait, she was, Tyrone decided, the most beautiful woman he'd ever seen, and possibly the most confident.

A lavish dinner was finished and they now were in the big sitting room dominated by the portraits of her ancestors.

"My daddy was an extraordinary man by anyone's measure, of course, but the greatness grew in him," she said proudly. "It was imposed by the fact that he was the inheritor of a great ranch. I have always held that a man becomes great by virtue of the challenges which are presented to him. People usually do not attribute greatness to a woman but I mean to match my father and to better him. I'm not being disrespectful or irreverent in saying this, believe me! My father created from what he inherited. Daddy built an important enterprise and no one can ever detract from that achievement. But there are going to be enormous changes in the years ahead, changes that this ranch must be able to meet head on. For example, I am looking toward the day when the railroads reach Texas. It is simply a matter of time. That will revolutionize the way we'll conduct the livestock business. I mean to be ready for that day. And when it comes, I want the Colter ranch to be the largest and mightiest there is. When people all over the country eat beef, I want it to come from the Colter ranch. I can even say that I'm looking forward to the day when no one will think of beef without thinking simultaneously of Texas and of Texas without thinking of the Colter brand." Her green eyes were glowing with excitement and her face was flushed. "I envision the day coming—sooner rather than later—in which we not only breed and raise cattle but handle the slaughtering, packing and shipping! Of course, all of this is still in the future—but not that far." She turned to Wofford, speaking insistently. "In the meantime, we require peace, law and order."

"The Rangers aim to provide it, ma'am," he said, looking and feeling as chastised as a rambunctious boy called to task by a school marm, Tyrone noted with amusement.

"When my granddaddy started in the cattle business all it took to become an owner was a rope, the nerve to use it and a branding iron," she continued proudly, her dark eyes flashing. "These days, things are not that easy. A rope, nerve and iron are still required but I can assure you that there's more to the livestock business than in that grand old man's day. Back then, the main part of the job was building the herd. Find 'em, catch 'em, put a brand on 'em." She paused and turned to Wofford. "It wasn't thieving, if that's what you're thinking, Lieutenant."

Now the Ranger looked startled, Tyrone thought.

"I assure you I wasn't, ma'am," said Wofford, shifting nervously.

"It's perfectly natural to think so," she went on, "and to perhaps wonder what makes the difference between my granddaddy grabbing cattle back in his day and the thieves who raid the ranges of the Nueces Strip today, but, you see, they were wild cattle. They belonged to nobody but God. They were free for the taking. Like it or not, that's the whole history of America, isn't it? Let's face it, Americans have grabbed the whole continent. In a sense, it's an entire country of thieves. We've taken from Indians. Mexicans. We're still taking, aren't we?"

"Seems so, ma'am," said Wofford dryly with one hand grasping a brandy glass and the other a cigar.

Rising, she boldly crossed the room to the bookcases where her grandfather's moroccan leather-bound journals stood in stolid, silent testimony to all of which she was heir. "In these volumes is the history of the past four decades on this part of Texas. I read in them the glorious annals of one man's personal quest for freedom and what he did to gain the independence of Texas. Someone else—a Mexican such as General Diaz, for instance—might find in these books a deplorable account of grab and greed. You might even easily make a case for the Texas War of Independence being nothing but a giant grab for land instead of what Texans claim it was, namely a fight for liberty. Rebellion is a question of your point of view. If you happen to be a rebel and win and that makes you a hero. If you lose, it makes you either dead or an exile."

"I know how that is," exclaimed her husband.

Tyrone thought he'd jumped in simply to end his wife's remarkable discourse.

"My late father was a rebel," said Morgan.

"I thought you were a born and bred Yankee, a Pennsylvanian," said Tyrone.

"Oh, I wasn't referring to the recent war! My dad's rebellion was years ago when he was a young man back in Wales. His side lost. That's how he came to come to America and to settle near Gettysburg where I was born." Looking down at the glass of brandy in his hands, he said, quietly, "That's where he died."

"In the battle?" asked Wofford.

"He was shot trying to keep the Rebs off the place. That was almost nine years ago. It's hard to believe."

Distantly, a baby cried.

"Our son Colt," said Morgan, his blue eyes lighting up with fatherly pride and shifting to his wife. "I expect he wants his mama."

"I'd best see to him," said Rebecca in a way that conveyed a feeling of irritation as Tyrone watched her turn and leave the room.

"She dotes on the kid," Morgan said proudly but unconvincingly as the child's wailing continued. "You'll meet him in the morning, when he'll be in a better mood!"

"We'll be ridin' on early," answered Wofford. "I'd like to make it to San Antone before night. Captain McNelly will be waitin', impatiently, I expect."

"I've yet to meet the captain," said Morgan, puffing his cigar. "I hear he's as tough as they come. That's just what we need these days—the strong arm of the law comin' down hard on these rustlers. We lost a dozen head last week down on the Nueces, killed for their hides and the carcasses left to rot. If the stealin' keeps up at that rate, there won't be many Colter beeves goin' up to Wichita in the spring."

Puzzled, Tyrone said, "They only took the hides? Why would they do that?"

"Around here the profit's in the skins and the tallow derived from them," said Morgan in a tone that was more patient than the angry blaze of his blue eyes. "All through the chaparral you'll find the remains of good beeves left to rot or be eaten by the coyotes and wild hogs. It's the Cortinistas who are behind it, raidin' across the Rio Grande and then scamperin' back to their lairs in Mexico, safe in the knowledge that neither the law nor the army on this side will go after 'em." He turned and pointed his cigar at Wofford. "That's why we ranchers are glad to see the Rangers takin' a hand." He glanced at Tyrone. "That'll make a dandy story for you to write!"

"I'm sure it would," said Tyrone, "but I believe Lieutenant Wofford's first assignment is to go after a knave called Saldana."

Morgan jerked his head approvingly. "That'll be good riddance to a bad penny."

"Ah, you've had some experience with him?" asked Tyrone.

"There's no rancher from Eagle Pass to Brownsville who hasn't! He's surely one of the worst examples of humanity ever to come down the pike. Murderer. Kidnapper. Woman beater. I called him for that once, as a matter of fact."

"Indeed?" said Wofford eagerly. "I hadn't heard."

"Our paths crossed about a year ago when ranch business took me to Crystal City, which is out by Espantosa

Lake, known as Saldana's stomping grounds. And a burial ground, according to some stories. Anyway, I was in a cantina and so was Saldana. He was with a young girl, a Mexican who worked in the place, and she said something snippy to him, whereupon he slapped her and would have given her a thorough thrashing if I hadn't intervened by drawing my gun on him. Coward that he is and not having his gang with him, he turned tail and ran. Had I shot him then and there, you, Lieutenant Wofford, would have been saved the trouble of tracking him down. I wish you luck in the endeavor. And you, Mr. Tyrone, I wish all success in your writings." He cracked a smile. "As long as you leave my name out of 'em."

SEVENTEEN

McNelly's Plan

The ruins of the old mission that won its immortality as a fortress were awash in pale moonlight.

"They held out against Santa Anna for twelve days," said Wofford in a husky, emotional voice. "If you want to understand Texans," he continued, clearing his throat, "you have to come to the Alamo." Stiffening, he rested his hand on the butt of his pistol. "All that they died for is not going to be surrendered now to the likes of the Saldana gang," he declared, "or anyone else who thinks he can ride roughshod over the law!"

They'd strolled to the Alamo from the Menger Hotel after a meal with the governor and Shanghai Pierce that had been lavish in its offerings and entertaining in its conversation. But it was ultimately disappointing because absent from the table was the one man Tyrone had been eagerly anticipating meeting since he'd first heard his name spoken by Wofford with such awe at El Rancho Grande—Captain Lee H. McNelly.

"He's been briefly detained on Rangers business in Austin," had been the governor's only explanation. "He'll join us in the morning."

"Maybe he's buyin' up a supply of those Winchester 73's," said Wofford hopefully as he led Tyrone to the Alamo while the governor and Shanghai retired to big leather chairs in a parlor of the hotel to smoke cigars and exercise the right to talk the rough-and-tumble politics of Texas that the martyrs of the Alamo had died to secure.

"You ought to give some thought to settlin' in Texas," said Wofford as they drifted away from the sight that had brought tears to his eyes. "We can always use more good men."

"Are you referring to the State or the Rangers?"

"Why, both, of course!"

At the meeting the next morning, Captain Lee McNelly was not at all what Tyrone expected. From the extravagant praise, even hero-worship, which had poured from Wofford's lips, he had expected to encounter a soldier of mythic proportions, but McNelly was a slight, sickly-looking man with a long, sallow and almost gaunt face that seemed stretched even farther by lengthy chin whiskers that all but obscured a drooping black bow tie more in keeping with the style of a businessman than a captain of the Texas Rangers.

Had Tyrone not been given the man's history by Wofford, he would never have believed that this frail, consumptive man had been a Confederate captain at the age of seventeen. A Virginian, he'd joined the flood of adventuring young men heading west at the end of the war and had been put in charge of a Ranger company, earning himself a reputation for efficiency despite the difficulties which Wofford had described as existing until Governor Coke came to office. Devoid of fear and favor, treating his men as social equals, he had won the devotion of his men that, judging by Wofford, Tyrone saw as approaching fanaticism.

"So this is the fellow who dealt so effectively with one

of the Ludlum cousins," McNelly said, greeting Tyrone with an iron-grip handshake. "My congratulations! Andy Wofford tells me you're a writer and that you've expressed an interest in our own little publication that the Rangers have taken to calling the Book of Knaves!"

"That sounds as if you'd give it a different title," answered Tyrone.

"Oh I would! I'd call it the Book of Losers. You see, young man, in the end they all will lose. Now this does not mean that we lawmen will always win. Far from it! We often lose. We don't fight to a draw. We win or we lose. But if we lose, we come back to fight again. And the law always wins the last round. As I believe Lieutenant Wofford has told you, we are about to step into the ring for a bout with the worst of these scoundrels—the murderous Mexican named Saldana. Would you care to help us?"

"I already explained to Andy that in spite of the Moe Ludlum incident, I'm not a gunfighter."

"Ah, but I don't want you to be a gunfighter! I want you to do what you apparently do best. I want you to gather information! You see, Tyrone, I am convinced that battles can be decided well before the first shot is fired . . . if you have garnered what the military calls intelligence. Lives can be saved and victories won if you have fresh, reliable information on your enemy. It's on this front that you can be most effective, by gathering information about the Saldana gang."

"Hold it," exclaimed Tyrone. "Are you asking me to spy?"

"Trust a newspaperman turned author to catch precisely the word I was looking for," laughed McNelly. "You're the ideal man! The wandering writer from back East who's combing the frontier for material for his next book! A man with an inquiring mind! Asking innocent questions! All the while soaking up everything he hears relevant to the Saldana gang. What could be better, eh?"

"Staying alive, for one thing!"

"Don't hand me that malarkey, Tyrone. The fellow who accompanied Marshal Mike Meagher in his search for the Ludlum boys, came face to face with Moe and lived to tell about it—or should I say 'write about it?'—is not a man to be intimidated by the possibility of his sudden demise! You're a young man I'd have been proud to have had with me in the war and honored to have serving with me as a Ranger. So, do me the service of at least considering my proposition."

"Assuming I might go for this idea of yours, what makes you think these people won't be suspicious of me and not clam up?"

"I know them! I've dealt with them before. You are correct in expecting them to be suspicious, but they will act in a way quite contrary to what you'd expect. They will do their best to find out about you. Rather than clam up, they will seek to probe you, find out who you are and what you're doing there."

"Okay, then what?"

"Eventually, the word of your presence will reach the ears of a local character by the name of John Fisher, better known in his domain as King," explained McNelly.

"The name rings a bell!"

"It's through King Fisher that I hope to pick up a lead on the whereabouts of the Saldana gang, for Fisher and Saldana are in cahoots. Indeed, there is nothing going on in Dimmit County, Texas, whether legal or illegal, that King Fisher doesn't have an interest in . . . and gets a cut of. If you accept my proposition and show up at Eagle Pass, sooner or later Fisher will be sending for you."

"And what on earth would prompt this King Fisher to want to see me?"

McNelly smiled and winked. "His ego! Fisher has a colossal ego. He's stuck on himself and has been all his life. He thinks of himself as the Napoleon of Dimmit County, ruling the roost like a banty rooster. If he thinks you can get his name in the newspapers, especially back East, and—better yet—write a book about him, he'll send for you."

"Great! And then what do I do? Ask him straight-out where his friend Saldana and his gang are?"

"If you think that'd do the trick," McNelly laughed.

"Captain, you take the cake!"

"But it's not the cake I want, my friend. I'm a captain and this is a war, and in a war, to the victor belongs the spoils. It's the spoils I want. The spoils of your meeting King Fisher will be the Saldana gang. I'm positive!"

A wagon road that began in San Antonio ran straight as an arrow into the shimmering heat of a high noon that tricked the eye into turning the flatlands surrounding Carrizo Springs into a mirage of a lake of rippling water. Beyond it on a low rise was a cluster of adobe buildings. Lifting his dusty hat, Wofford wiped sweat from his brow. "Not much to speak of, eh?"

"If they got a place where a man can wet his whistle," said Tyrone, "it'll suit me just fine."

Wofford clapped his hat on. "I'm afraid you're out of luck, my friend. Carrizo Springs is dry as a bone."

"No liquor?"

"Nary a drop."

"Is there a law against it or something?"

"In a way. You might call it King Fisher's law. He's a teetotaler and has decreed that there'll be no spirits in the town; no saloons or drinking."

"Ridiculous!"

"Don't worry," laughed Wofford. "There's a cantina farther up the road at a place called Espantosa, but I doubt if they stock your brand of whiskey."

"The local brand'll do fine."

"It's likely to be mescal. That's a Mexican brew that'll either put hair on your chest or burn it off."

Baking in the sun, the cantina was an adobe block with one door and one window and a bar that consisted of a plank stretched between stacked barrels.

As mescal after mescal burned down his throat and set his head spinning delightfully, Tyrone listened to Wofford's sober discourse on the subject of King Fisher.

"I suppose the event that first made Fisher's reputation was one day over in Zavala County," he began. "The story is that he and a gang of Mexican cattle thieves were dividing up the spoils and the Mexicanos got it into their heads that Fisher was pullin' a fast one. Well, the King figured they might be plannin' on killin' him. But he didn't let on he suspected 'em. He just kept brandin' and watchin' 'em out of the corner of his eye. And just as they made their move, he sprang into action. He brained the closest one with a brandin' iron and, smooth as good whiskey, he drew and gunned down three others, pickin' 'em off a fence like they was roostin' birds."

"So how come he wasn't prosecuted?"

"First off, the victims were Mexicans. Second, he lit out to a favorite hideout of his, which is a cave somewhere along the Nueces that the law has never located. He buried himself there for a time, letting the stink blow over—which wasn't long because, as I say, they were Mexicans and Texans are inclined to overlook the killin' of Mexicans, especially bandits. And the whole thing made Fisher into a kind of hero, for after that he ranged from the Nueces to the Chicon, from Eagle Pass to Carrizo Springs. Now he's the king of that territory and a sort of godfather of all that goes on illegally. The result is that he's built himself a pretty sizeable empire that owes its existence to lawlessness. He's not just a king of the cattle trade. He's a king of bandits. They all find a welcome at his spread down by the Pendencia Creek. That's why Captain McNelly believes that if you can worm your way close to him we'll get a line on where to find Saldana. The captain's right about Fisher havin' an exalted opinion of himself. Believe me, my friend, once he gets wind of a book-writin' fella askin' about him, he'll show up lookin' for you in Eagle Pass in all his glory! When he does, all you have to do is find out from him how to get to Hezekiah."

"Is that all?"

Wofford grinned. "And then you can hightail it to our bivouac at Carrizo Springs and tell us. Of course, if you decide at that point to come along while we wipe out the Saldana gang, I'd be pleased to have your charmin' company."

"You makc it all sound so easy!"

"Why not? I'm a Texas Ranger, after all!"

EIGHTEEN

Eagle Pass

The trail which Wofford plotted for Tyrone was a rutted wagon road running straight west from Carrizo Springs for twenty miles to a lonely slash-in-the-scrub-and-brush town known as El Indio, which was all of three sun-bleached wooden buildings and a handful of men who looked at him with silent suspicion. Passing through slowly but without stopping, he slanted northwest parallel to the Rio Grande for another fifteen under a sun unimpeded by clouds and surrounded by the heat of it shimmering above the parched ground like layers of rippling water.

But this hard land that any man in his senses would have called godforsaken teemed with life—a wild boar sow snorting across the trail with two babies scampering behind, jackrabbits darting in and out of the crackling scrub, a wild turkey running for cover, birds he didn't know what to call flurrying skyward in flocks that circled noisily before diving out of sight again and all manner of crawling things scampering in the dirt—scorpions, tarantulas and vinegaroons among them—and plenty of snakes that coiled and rattled as he passed or slithered silently into hiding. But, amazingly, for what he knew to be cattle country, he saw not one of the animals.

For his sake and Redskin's in the wilting heat of what he had to remind himself was winter, he proceeded slowly, rocking gently in the saddle and almost lulled to sleep more than once.

By late afternoon a sheet of white washboard clouds was blocking the sun and a breeze had come up coolingly.

Then, quite abruptly, he found himself coming across a rise and looking down on a sleepy cluster of structures nudging the sun-flaked brown flow of the Rio Grande. "Well, Redskin," he said, stroking the horse's coat, "I suppose that has to be Eagle Pass."

During the war with Mexico, a small contingent of American soldiers camping north of the Rio Grande had noticed the daily flight of an eagle back and forth across the Rio Grande to its nest in a towering cottonwood tree on the Mexican side and, consequently, named their post after it—Camp Eagle Pass. In 1849, the place became a way-station on the route to the gold fields of California and the following year a little town was laid out—*El Paso de Aguila.* In the Civil War it was part of a circuitous route around the Union blockade of seaports for Confederate cotton being shipped to Europe. Some say it was at Eagle Pass that the war truly ended when, on the morning of July 4, 1865, General Joseph O. Shelby marshalled his 500 veterans around their battle flag, gave it a last salute and lowered it, weighted, into the muddy Rio Grande—the last flag to fly over an unsurrendered Confederate force, leading to the veneration of the spot as the Grave of the Confederacy.

The seat of Dimmit County, Eagle Pass in 1874 attracted settlers who came to record their deeds and, as the western anchor of the rustler-plagued Nueces Strip, drew cattlemen to register their brands. Because it was the gateway to Mexico, it was also a magnet for those who were attempting to flee the law either in Mexico or Texas—the knaves being sought by McNelly's Rangers.

The Old Blue Saloon had been elegant in those boisterous, rushing hell-bent for California Gold Rush days when Eagle Pass was flourishing and prosperous, but when Tyrone walked in, it was long past its prime.

Flocked red wallpaper had faded pink and was soiled from two decades of smoke from lamps and tobacco. Gilt trim on the ceiling had lost its glint. A brass rail that once must have been the pride of the long bar was dented, scuffed, scratched and tarnished dark brown in spots from being stepped on by the countless thousands of boots that also wore the paint off the wooden flooring and smoothed footpaths in the bared boards from the doors to the bar.

Where untold customers had stood shoulder to shoulder gulping uncounted gallons of liquor, circular indentations had been slowly gouged in the flooring and the sheen of the rich mahogany bar itself was turning bald at the spots where all those elbows had been propped.

A dozen chairs and tables stood pitted from the rowels of spurs where men had plunked their feet. Three rows of brass lamps dangled from the ceiling, their glass chimneys and shades crusted black from years of soot.

At the rear of the room curved a grand staircase leading to a balcony. Evenly spaced along the balcony were doors to rooms for the convenience of patrons preferring privacy. Faded and worn down to a frazzle, a red carpet with golden embroidering at its edges covered the staircase that must have known the delicate tread of women's shoes as well as the clump of boots of women-starved men going up to the rooms.

An upright piano occupied a nook in the wall opposite the bar and now, as it must have been since it was installed so many years ago. It was being played, although with much more enthusiasm than artistry by a Mexican who either did not care that the instrument was out of tune or didn't know it.

Its tinniness was dampened by the babbling of at least two dozen patrons scattered along the bar and at the tables, a mixture of men from both sides of the border, their conversations punctuated by the laughter of four women.

Judged by Tyrone to be the type who would not be shy about climbing the stairway's faded carpet, they turned their heads and solicitous eyes to scrutinize him as he bellied up to the bar to be eyed with curiosity by a burly young bartender with a handlebar mustache, a white apron stretched tight around his ample midsection and an age-old question. "Whatcha drinkin'?"

"Mescal," said Tyrone, hopeless that there might be Irish whiskey amidst the unlabeled bottles lining a shelf behind the bar.

"I ain't seen you before," said the bartender, pouring.

"Never been here before. This town *is* Eagle Pass?"

"None other."

"Well it sure is a long way from anywhere, isn't it?"

"I never been nowhere else so I wouldn't know about that."

"Ah, you've lived here your entire life?"

"Born and bred."

"Then I reckon you're the very man for me to talk to. My name's Tyrone and I've made my way down here from New York. I'm a newspaperman sent by my editor, Mr. James Gordon Bennett, for the purpose of writing some articles about the people and the towns along the border with Mexico. Now, here I am, talking to a man who's lived in these parts all his years. I guess that's the luck of the Irish, eh?"

"First time I ever heard anybody say that bein' in Eagle Pass was lucky. You're plannin' to stay awhile, is that it?"

"Well, I just arrived and really haven't given much thought to how long I might linger. Fact is, this establishment is the first place I stopped. My experience has taught me that the best way to get the layout of a new place is at the local watering hole. Nobody sees more, hears more and knows more than the fellow who slings the liquor, right?"

"That's for sure," grinned the flattered bartender.

"Wet the whistle first, then see about the rest of it; that's my way of things when I enter a new town."

"You're obviously a man who knows his priorities!"

"Can you recommend a hotel?"

"There's only one, to the left as you step outside, on the other side of the street."

"A livery?"

"Fulmer's. A little ways on."

"Gotta see that your horse is taken care of properly, you know," said Tyrone, turning slightly toward the women. "Those gals look mighty pretty."

"They're available, if that's what you're wonderin'."

Slapping a half dollar on the bar, Tyrone smiled. "I'll be back later."

"They'll be here."

At Fulmer's livery a Negro boy with a toothy grin took charge of Redskin, happily pocketing extra money Tyrone gave him as a tip for the tending of the saddle. "Don't worry, boss," he said. "It be as good as new when I'm done."

The lobby of the hotel looked used, presided over by a gray-haired clerk wearing a green eye shade and black sleeve garters. "Room six, second floor," he said as Tyrone signed a register. "The bath house is out back."

Yellow with the light of the setting sun, the big bedroom that matched the number on the brass key was in front with a bay window that afforded a view of the quiet street from the end that led to the river and Mexico and the hard-baked road he'd come in on from Carrizo Springs. Stretching out on a huge four poster bed with an unforgiving stiff horsehair mattress, he tried to sleep, tossing and turning for nearly an hour before giving up and returning to the Old Blue, wondering if by chance he might encounter King Fisher.

The same bartender greeted him with a nod of recognition and a brimming shot of mescal. "Did you get yourself all set?"

"Save for something to eat," said Tyrone, patting his belly. "Where's a body get some vittles around here?"

"We got a Chinee cook if you don't mind refried beans and burnt beef."

"Well, I'll tell you . . . what's your name, by the way?"

"Jake."

"I'm Tyrone. As I was saying, it's been so long since I ate, my belly thinks my throat's been cut, so even Mexican chow whipped up by a Chinaman will be just fine."

Leaving the bottle of mescal and heading toward a door that Tyrone presumed led to a kitchen or a cookhouse, Jake said, "It'll be a few minutes."

"Waited this long, a little more won't hurt," said Tyrone, turning to survey the room.

In the absence of the piano player, a half-dozen men produced their own music, a rumbling baritone pierced now and then by the laughter of a pair of women, teasing and being teased as they kibbitzed a quartet worrying over five card stud.

His eyes met those of one of the girls he'd seen earlier, a glance that she took as a signal. Leaving the man, she picked her way through the thicket of unoccupied tables. Looking no more than sixteen, she had widely set dark eyes, a defiant chin and brown hair that hung in long braids across the front of a white blouse worn open to reveal the swell and sway of large breasts. A green skirt cascaded from wide hips and swirled around her legs as she crossed the room, catlike in moccasins. "I saw you in here before but you left," she said. "I'm Magdalena. Buy me a drink?"

"Soon as Jake comes back."

"I can get my own," she smiled, swirling behind the bar and helping herself to a bottle of rye. "He won't mind. I do it all the time. Sometimes if it's busy I even help out servin' the drinks."

"I'll bet you sell a lot of liquor," he said, teasingly as he helped himself to more mescal. "This is my second, in case you're keeping count for the house."

Jake returned bearing a plate heaped with cooked beans and a steaming steak blackened around the edges. "You eatin' this at the bar, a table or . . ." He winked at Magdalena. ". . . up in one of the rooms?"

"A table," said Tyrone, taking the plate. "I never mix my pleasures."

That she would go with him to his hotel room and stay the night was not brought up until nearly midnight when he decided he'd had enough of playing losing poker while fruitlessly eavesdropping for mentions of King Fisher and Saldana, settled his bar bill with Jake, turned to her and asked, "Whatcha say, Maggie? Shall we?"

"You're a funny one," she said, taking his arm as they left the saloon. "You're nothin' like other men I been with."

"That so?" he answered, smoking a cheroot as they walked toward the hotel. "In what way am I different?"

"You never say to me, 'Magdalena, we will be together later. Please wait for me.' I could have gone with another man, you know."

"But you didn't."

"You don't ask how much money I charge."

"I'm sure you'll be fair."

"You play cards all night and never get mad when you lose."

"I never lose more than I'm prepared to."

"You drink and don't get drunk."

"I know what it takes to make me drunk and stop before I get there. What else did you notice about me?"

"You pretend to be mindin' your own business and all the time you are payin' attention to everythin' that is goin' on around you."

"Is that so?"

"I watch you. And I ask myself, 'Who is this stranger with the big ears?' "

Taking the cheroot from his mouth, he stopped short and tugged at his left ear. "They are not big! They're just the right size. Ladies like my ears just the way they are. They have even been known to call them cute! Like handles on tea cups, one lady once said to me concerning them."

"I meant they are big in hearing. Like a wolf's! You were listenin' to everythin' that was bein' said. It made me think you were a spy."

"Ha! A spy! What a hoot!" He walked on, holding her hand. "Whose spy?"

Now she stopped, thrusting fists against her hips. "How should I know whose spy? I don't know nothin' about spies, 'cept that a lot of the men who come to town are always talkin' about the Texas Rangers sendin' in men to snoop around lookin' for bandits and rustlers. That's spyin' ain't it? I thought maybe you were a spy like that."

"The only thing in this town that I spied," he said, stroking her arm, "is you. Truth to tell, the only thing of any interest to me at all since I rode in was you."

She laughed deep in her throat. "Ah, I knew you liked me soon as I laid eyes on you. 'Magdalena,' I said, 'there is a man for you.' "

"That's great," he said, pulling her to him. "Then you can pay me!" He seized her round the waist. "How much you give? A peso?" Tickling her, he laughed, "Two peso? Five?" He whirled away from her. "Twenty?"

"You crazy," she yelled.

Cavorting like a clown, he skipped into the deserted street. "How about a hundred?"

"You not worth a hundred pesos," she giggled, chasing him.

"Not pesos," he shouted, bounding onto the hotel boardwalk. "A hundred *dollars!*"

NINETEEN

Rude Awakening

"You are funny," she said, kissing his left ear.

"That's 'cause I'm a leprechaun," he giggled, tickled.

She was at his right ear now, nibbling and whispering into it in moist gusts, "I never knew nobody as different as you. You treat me like I was a lady."

Long ago, he remembered, one of the newspapermen hanging out at McGlory's Garden of Eden had told him, "The way to succeed with the women folk, lad, is to treat a whore like a lady and a lady like a whore."

The memory brought Peggy Doyle to mind. And Crazy Sid shoving her around, pushing her to the floor. And plunging against Sid, arms flailing wildly, wanting to punish him for not treating Peggy like a lady. Then a gun coming out of nowhere, struggling for it. The gun going off, killing Sid.

He'd not seen Peggy Doyle since and wondered where she was at that moment and what she might say if she knew the part she had played in his life, how because of her his entire life had been changed.

Why had he rushed to help her? he wondered. Surely, she'd been pushed around by other men, possibly many times by Sid, and no one had gone to her aid. Why had he? It would have been easy to have turned away. All had, except those who relished a good fight of any sort. Yet outrage had risen in him like a sudden flood. And he was still being carried by that tide, swept all the way to the farthest end of Texas, his life transformed forever.

"Whatchoo thinkin' about?" said Magdalena, rising over him and grinning down at him out of her round, brown face.

"About how cruel men can be," he answered.

"Not you," she laughed. "You are . . . gentle. You treat a girl with respect, not the way some men do. They are pigs. That's what I call them. Pig men. The ones who like to beat up girls."

"Who beat you up, Maggie?" he said, stroking the long brown hair that tumbled across her breasts. "Give me their names and I'll beat them up for you."

"Killin's what they deserve. Especially the one called Saldana."

"Saldana?"

"He beat me bad once."

"Which one is he? Is he at the Old Blue? Point him out to me and I'll kill him for you."

"He is gone now. There are wanted posters with his name on them. Big reward! No one will ever find him. He's hidin' in the hills."

"Do you know where? Tell me where he's hiding out and I'll make him pay for beating you."

"No one knows where. And if anyone does, he won't say. All the people are afraid of Saldana."

"I'm not!"

"Forget Saldana," she said, falling on him demandingly.

He might have slept with her through the morning but for the racketing of gunfire below his hotel room window jolting him awake.

Rolling from bed and peering cautiously out, he observed a tall, lean Mexican on a painted horse racing from one end of the street to the other and back again, firing into the air apparently just for the fun of it until he jerked the horse to a stop in front of the Old Blue, bounded down, tied up the horse and strode inside.

Naked, the girl had joined Tyrone at the window. "That's Pancho announcing his presence," she said, yawning and stretching. "He's a showoff."

"Yeah? What's he got to show off about?"

"He thinks that just because he's King Fisher's right-hand man that he's somethin' himself," she said, returning to the bed.

"I've heard about this King Fisher," said Tyrone, leaving the window to lie beside her. "They say he calls all the shots around here."

"That's right."

"Ever meet him?"

"Oh, you bet," she giggled. "All the girls at Old Blue know the King. He's very good looking and very rich and he's not rough and mean like the others, like Saldana. Neither are you. You both are gentle with a girl. You're a lot like the King but different in other ways. You talk funny. You're not a Texan, I can tell that from the way you talk. Are you also a rich man?"

"Hardly. And not likely to be."

"Why not? King Fisher wasn't always rich. If he can do it why shouldn't you?"

"If he's so rich, why don't you marry him?"

"Men like him don't marry girls like me."

"I'll tell you what. If I ever meet this King Fisher, I'll tell him he's missing a good bet by not marrying you. How's that?"

"Sweet," she said, kissing him, "but I won't hold my breath."

"That's good, 'cause I probably won't ever meet Fisher."

"Stay around Eagle Pass and you're bound to."

"He comes to town a lot?"

"Regular as a clock. He told me once that he likes to keep up on things. He said to me, 'I make it my business to know everythin' that goes on.' And that's what he does when he comes to town, askin' who's doin' what, who's in town and for what reason, who's askin' about him and why. So I expect if you hang around for awhile he'll come round checkin' you out, too."

The piano was clanging again when Tyrone returned to the Old Blue that evening, noting that the card game that seemed to go on endlessly had been joined by the man Magdalena had identified as Pancho. Noticing an empty chair and after collecting a mescal from Jake, he eased close to the players. "Is this a private game or can anybody join in?" he asked.

Pancho looked up through yellowed eyes that were no more than slits. "The ante's a buck," he said. "Coin, not foldin'. If you got it, we got nothin' against takin' it away from you."

Thrusting a hand into a pocket, Tyrone jiggled his coins. "Sounds like eagles in there to me," he grinned.

Hooking a boot heel on a rung of the empty chair and sliding it back, Pancho said, "Have a seat, Tyrone. That is your handle, ain't it?"

Unable to mask his surprise, Tyrone dropped heavily into the chair, but recovery was quick. "That's it." He flashed a grin. "And yours is Pancho, I believe. Right-hand man to King Fisher?"

"That's the trouble with this town," grumbled the Mexican as he gathered the cards from the previous hand and slid a sidelong accusing glance toward Magdalena. "Everybody talks too much. A man can't go about his business without everybody stickin' a nose in."

"Shooting-up the main street does attract attention, Pancho. Your doing it certainly got mine. I wanted to know who it was that rousted me out of bed, so don't hold it against her just because she was kind enough to tell me the name of the fellow that was doing it."

Pancho grinned, revealing a checkerboard of tarnished white and gleaming gold top teeth. "Let me tell you this, amigo," he roared. "There ain't no amount of shootin' in the street that could roust me outta that one's bed!"

"Well, I guess I'm the curious type."

Pancho shuffled the cards. "A newspaperman is what I hear you are."

Tyrone glanced to the bar and at Jake. "The only creature on God's earth that's more talkative than a woman," he said, smiling, "is a saloon keeper."

Dealing five card stud, Pancho asked, "What's your interest in the King?"

Tyrone picked up a losing hand. "Powerful men make interesting reading."

"And what if he don't want people readin' about him?"

"Then that's that, I suppose," said Tyrone, folding.

The others followed.

With a winner's smirk, Pancho raked in the pot.

"The thing of it is," said Tyrone as the deck passed to him for dealing, "I'd like to hear King tell me first-hand that I'm wasting my time."

"He's a busy man."

"I'd be surprised if he wasn't," said Tyrone, dealing. "On the other hand, I'm not going anywhere in a hurry. Fact is, I've got nothing but time on my hands. And I'm a very patient fellow." Studying the hand he'd dealt himself, he found winning cards, but Pancho, he decided, was a man who looked as if he did not like losing. "I'm out," he said, throwing in the hand.

Pancho grinned. "What did you say your name was?"

"Tyrone," said he, winning again.

"TIE-RONE."

"An easy name to remember."

TWENTY

The King

The silence that engulfed the Old Blue with the arrival of King Fisher was as complete as the moment when the police arrived after the shooting of Crazy Sid in the Garden of Eden. He'd expected an older man, but John King Fisher advancing his way looked to be no older than himself—in his twenties—yet if all the stories about him were true, he was the monarch of all he surveyed.

Tall and handsome with black eyes and black hair and mustache, he wore a broad-brimmed sombrero ornamented with gold and silver lace and a golden snake for a band. A fine buckskin Mexican short jacket heavily embroidered with gold was open to reveal a fine linen shirt open at the throat and with a silk handkerchief knotted loosely about the wide collar. Around his waist was tied a brilliant crimson sash. Supple leather chaps covered denim pants. Black blunt-toed boots looked new. His spurs were of silver and ornamented with little silver bells. A silver-studded gunbelt supported a brace of ivory-handled Colt six-guns. "My friends tell me that you expressed an interest in meetin' me," he said without preliminaries. "Somethin' about wantin' to write me up in some newspaper. I've always had an admiration for men who have a knack for words but none ever came round expressin' an interest in me before."

"Their mistake . . . and misfortune," said Tyrone amiably. "I've heard that you've had a pretty interesting life."

"Where'd you hear that?"

"In every saloon in the Nueces Strip."

"It's a good yarn," said Fisher, grinning and tipping back his sombrero. "It's even better the way I tell it."

"I'm eager to hear it."

Fisher studied him hard, the black eyes penetrating like drills. "Yeah, I see that you are. Anyone who throws away a winnin' hand in a poker game on the chance that it might lead to a meetin' with me is pretty eager."

"Where'd you get that crazy notion?"

"Oh, it ain't a notion. It's a fact. Accordin' to Pancho, you were holdin' three aces. And he ought to know. It was his deck. Marked, of course. Now why would a man deliberately lose? I figure it was because you didn't want to beat Pancho's hand and make him upset, thus queerin' any chance of him carryin' your name to me. Pretty smart. But Pancho would have told me about you even if he did lose, 'cause his only purpose in bein' in town that day was to check you out."

Tyrone shot a glance at Jake behind the bar. "Nothing gets past you, eh?"

"When someone's askin' about me I like to know of it right away."

"Like I said, you're an interesting fellow."

"Folks augurin' about me in the barrooms of the Strip is one thing," Fisher said, shifting his glance to the patrons surrounding them, "but what in dickens makes you think people back East would care to read about me?"

"The folks back East are interested in everything about the frontier."

"Why's that?"

"They find it exciting."

"If it's so excitin' why don't they come out and see for themselves?"

"I expect it's mostly a lack of nerve on their part."

"Nerve's somethin' you've got in spades, eh?"

"When you're out of a job, nerve is secondary. I'd just been fired from mine. So when the book publishing firm of Beadle and Adams made me an offer to come out here to find interesting people to write books about, I grabbed it, nerves notwithstanding. So far, you're the most interesting person I've run across."

"Is that a fact?"

"I've come a long way to meet you, so I'll be sharply disappointed if you were to hand me my walking papers. And think of the thrilling reading the folks back East will be denied if I have to pack up and move on, knowing I'll never find a better yarn than that of King Fisher no matter how far I travel!"

Fisher thought a long time before saying, "The tellin' of my experiences could take a bit of time."

"If a good story's at stake, time's the one thing I have in abundance."

"What is it you'd want to know?"

"The whole kit and kaboodle. The full story of how you got to be the man folks call King of the Pendencia."

"That's mighty flatterin'."

"Isn't it the truth?"

"I won't deny that I've earned a certain amount of respect in these parts."

Tyrone's eyes drifted through the crowded, noisy room. "Is there a quieter place where we could continue this conversation?"

Slapping Tyrone's back, Fisher laughed. "Like the parlor of my house, for instance? There's nothin' very subtle about you, is there, Tyrone?"

"I've got plenty of faults, but being indirect is not one of them."

TWENTY-ONE

The King's Story

He was born in Collin County, Texas, the first child of Jobe Fisher and the former Lucinda Warren, Fisher began as they mounted their horses. "They were hard-shell Baptists." A grin of memory was more wince than smile. "I recall when we was livin' in Florence that my brother Jasper and me got whaled by our pop for helpin' ourselves to some forbidden plums from a neighbor's thicket. I reckon I was about seven at the time." He winked mischievously. "Would you say that was a foretellin' that I was headed for a life on the distant side of the law?"

"Every kid steals."

"The worst scrape of my growin' up was when I was fifteen and accused of swipin' a horse."

"Accused? Does that mean you didn't swipe it?"

"Well, not at first. I borrowed it at first. It was later circumstances that turned the borrowin' into a case of stealin'. You see, I'd been out ridin' and decided to take a nap. While I was sleepin', my own hoss slipped away. So I borrowed a stallion belongin' to a Mr. Turnbow. It was a right pretty horse and Turnbow fancied it quite a lot. The truth is, I was goin' to return that stallion but when I found out that Turnbow'd sworn out a warrant, well, I took off. A jailhouse never figured in any of my plans, you see?"

"That's an understandable attitude to adopt," muttered Tyrone.

"The upshot was, I was caught the next mornin' . . . asleep again . . . and hauled off to the pokey. But . . ." He snorted a laugh and drew his horse to a halt. "But get this; Turnbow had a change of heart about prosecutin' me and slips a little knife to me to cut the rope they had on me—which I promptly did. I hightailed it to Goliad and never went back to Florence. But things soon got hot in Goliad. It was a housebreakin' charge this time." He nudged his big yellow horse forward, still at a walk. "The good people of Goliad were on a toot against what they called the lawless element at that time. Feelin's were runnin' high and I got the brunt of it—two years sentence in the penitentiary. I was but sixteen years old."

"That's pretty young to be slammed into prison."

"That's what the governor thought, 'cause I was given a full pardon and sprung. Naturally, I had no further taste for the do-gooders of Goliad . . ."

"Naturally!"

". . . so I lit out lookin' for a buddy of mine who was also ridin' the owlhoot trail at the time, a fella by the name of Charlie Bruton. I heard he'd headed down this way and that was good enough for me.

"He'd found it a lawless territory where Mexican bandits operated from nests south of the Rio Grande, raiding across the border to steal livestock, augmented by packs of Indians on the warpath. They were Lipans, Kiowas, Comanches, and Apaches, which was a handful for anybody," he went on. "But there was also your run of the mill thieves and desperadoes from up north who made it their business to plague the settlers. So with all that happenin' nobody was interested in my pissant past. All they cared about was havin' another hand to fight the outlaws and redskins. That's when I learned to shoot with both hands, taught by one of the slickest gunmen in the territory, a mean half-breed Mexican by the name of Saldana."

"Seems to me I've heard of him," said Tyrone in a tone as casual as he could create.

"It's a name that strikes fear," chuckled Fisher. "Refugio Gonzales Ruis Saldana, known by some as the butcher of Carrizo Springs on account of his cuttin' off the ears and nose of an enemy after a knock-down-and-drag-out fist fight in the local waterin' hole. Naturally the ruckus was over a woman. Ol' Saldana's always had an eye peeled for somethin' pretty in skirts."

Eagle Pass was far behind them now, the sun was sliding down low and Tyrone was adding up all that he'd heard from McNelly, Wofford, Morgan and Fisher himself into a picture of a cunning young man who had parlayed his winning personality, gunmanship, aggressiveness and opportunity into an empire straddling the Mexican border and the line between law and illegality.

They'd come, now, to a fork.

Beside the right-turning road stood a large sign that seemed to sum up the young man on the big yellow horse:

THIS IS KING FISHER'S ROAD!
TAKE THE OTHER ONE.

"That's blunt," said Tyrone.

"Meant to be," said Fisher.

Passing it, they proceeded a mile with no buildings of his ranch yet in view as Fisher set a slow pace, clearly enjoying relating a history remarkably close to the one Wofford had told, amounting to a portrait of a young man hell-bent for excitement and derring-do whose smooth friendliness and winning qualities had allowed him to become surrounded by well-wishers and admirers from both sides of the law.

As if Fisher had timed it for effect, their plodding horses crested a small hill at the moment the setting sun was flaring its last burst of yellow light to gild the whitewashed walls of an adobe ranch house under a meandering, gently sloped roof of orange-colored tiles.

Taken by the sight himself, Fisher reined up, took his time lighting a cigarette and, smiling proudly, asked, "Pretty, ain't it?"

TWENTY-TWO

Ghost Stories

Shouldered up against the Mexican border, the Pendencia Creek area of Dimmit County was a lush prairie of tall grass, babbling brooks and scenic grandeur that invited settlement in the years immediately after the Civil War. Those who pioneered it built houses copied from the huts of Mexican pastores with walls made of posts or pickets of the mesquite and elm that abounded along the banks of the creek, but King Fisher's home was a palace by comparison and as lavish as Shanghai Pierce's Casa Blanca.

Supper was served outdoors on a breezy veranda lit by hanging paper lanterns and chimneyed candles in silver holders, delivered by Pancho, who was older than Fisher, although when they spoke to one another the tone was as if their ages were reversed.

"This place was nothin' when I first set foot on it, right, Pancho?" said Fisher as the Mexican poured cups of steaming, strong coffee.

"Nothin' but chaparral and rattlesnakes," Pancho replied.

"Things were wide open and free for the takin'," said

Fisher, stretching out his arms as if he were about to gather all he surveyed. "The land was crawlin' with cattle and horses, most strays, a few not! With a little effort, a man could round 'em up and deliver 'em at ten dollars a head to drovers who were collectin' for the big drives. There was also a good market for Spanish mustangs. Roundin' up the beeves was business. But catchin' and tamin' those hosses was the real thrill. The one I was ridin' this afternoon was one of the ones I tamed. I call him Old Yaller. That hoss can pace a mile a minute. Your mount looked mighty fine, too."

"I call him Redskin."

"Ever race him?"

"Nope, but not because I think Redskin couldn't handle it. I'd be the one who'd be left at the post."

Chewing on a cigar, Fisher smiled around it. "I'd bet that nothin' ever left you behind!"

The following two days were more of the same as Fisher seemed to grow more relaxed and trusting, enjoying spinning yarns about himself, all of them harmless tales of teenage pranks and scrapes with authorities with no further mention of Saldana. Through all of it, whether listening to Fisher's ramblings at the table, on the veranda or as they rode the range on Old Yaller and Redskin, Tyrone felt that he was being measured and weighed less and less.

At breakfast on the third day, Fisher came in dressed for riding. "Eat up fast, Tyrone," he said. "I got somethin' special to show you, a place only a few of my most trusted friends know about."

Riding north at a brisk pace, he said nothing more concerning their destination until they reached the lip of a deep cut in the land formed by the Nueces River. "Best to hike it from here," he said, dismounting and leading his horse toward the dense brush and thickets that sloped steeply toward the snaking, muddy river far below. Halfway down, he stopped to look round and announce, "This is it."

Baffled, Tyrone grunted "This is . . . what?" and followed Fisher until, quite suddenly, he found himself in a clearing as flat as a table in front of the mouth of a cave.

"Whatcha think?" beamed Fisher.

A study in puzzlement, Tyrone muttered, "What is it?"

"Mine and Saldana's old hideout," answered Fisher, striding into the cave standing up.

"Lordy, look at this," gasped Tyrone, following him.

Fisher lit a torch to reveal a space as roomy as a dance hall cut deep into the hillside with walls as smooth as plaster rising twice his height before slanting to form a domed ceiling that nature had equipped with an opening that formed a natural chimney for the black smoke curling up from Fisher's light.

In the center of the floor were the blackened remains of fires and around that circle of ashes, small boulders and slabs of rocks had been made into benches. Neatly aligned at the foot of the back wall as Tyrone explored were half a dozen buckets. Covered and tightly tied with rawhide, they contained an assortment of dried beans. Hanging from nails driven into the wall were several water canteens, firmly capped and full.

"Saldana showed me this place," said Fisher. "He said it was the perfect hideout and he was right, although he doesn't use it anymore."

"How come?" Tell me about Saldana, he thought. Where is he? How can I get to him? Will you take me to him?

"He's set himself up a lot better'n this at a spot called Hezekiah. It's a hidden valley nearby Turkey Mountain just past the fork of the Nueces beyond Uvalde. That's a fortress compared to this. You should see it."

"I'd like to," Tyrone said blandly.

Fisher dipped a hand into one of the buckets and

scooped up shiny white beans. "They're still as fresh as the day Sally and I put 'em here. This cave is real dry. The dryness keeps them." The beans drained through his fingers like water and sounded like rain on a tin roof as they piled up. "Saldana doesn't exactly welcome visitors."

Light-heartedly, Tyrone said, "Not even escorted by an old saddle buddy?"

Fisher cracked a grin. "It'd be a hoot to see him again and he'd prob'ly get a boot out of the notion of me bein' immortalized in a book."

"He'll be in it, too, of course," said Tyrone. "Maybe that would appeal to him?"

"There's no question that Sally could give you some pretty hair-raisin' stories," said Fisher, lighting lanterns that turned the cave as bright as daylight. "But all in all, I don't know how he'd take to sharin' 'em with a stranger. He's never been as trustin' as yours truly."

"I guess I can see it from his side," said Tyrone, deciding not to press too hard, "but from my end, it sure would be good to hear what Saldana has to say about the days when he was teamed up with King Fisher."

"We were a hell of team, that's for sure," said Fisher, sitting on one of the stone benches. "We've both got a lot to answer for on Judgment Day, I expect."

Tyrone sat leaning forward with his fingers linked loosely and looking at Fisher out of the tops of his eyes. "Including killings?"

"A lot less than I've been credited with, believe me. But I did kill a few."

"How many's a few?"

"Six, not countin' Mexicans. Sally's toll is higher. The shootin's I have to answer for were all justified—bandidoes, rustlers and the like. The ones I had to kill were deservin' of it."

"Saldana's weren't?"

"Well, I can't answer for him, but I always thought Sally kind of enjoyed it when he drew on a man."

"When's the last time you saw him?"

"Let's see; a couple a months ago, mebbe. I ran into him in Eagle Pass. He was the same old pisser as always. He wound up pistol-whippin' one of the customers at the Old Blue Saloon over a Mexican girl by the name of Evangeline. Hell of a handle for a senorita, huh? Pretty thing, of course. Sally likes 'em pretty . . . and young. They put out a wanted notice for him that listed the charge as kidnappin'." He paused, poking a toe into the long-dead campfire. "I always predicted that it would be a woman that'd be his downfall. His trouble is he can't live without 'em and don't know how to treat 'em. His way of expressin' himself to a female is to slam her around. Sally says women like it. I used to say to him, 'Sally, one of these days some woman's gonna plant a knife in your heart.' Anyway, he took that girl Evangeline with him and now he's got a kidnappin' charge hangin' over him."

"Speaking of women, how about you? Is there a queen in the king's future?"

Fisher's eyes lit up. "Her name's Sarah Vivian."

Tyrone grinned. "Gonna marry her?"

"Mebbe," said Fisher, bolting out of the cave.

Before he spoke again, the sun was directly overhead and glinting hard off the smooth surface of a long narrow lake. "They call this place Espantosa," Fisher declared, reining in Old Yaller. "The ghost lake! Some people say it's full of alligators, though I never encountered one." Fishing the makings from his shirt pocket, he rolled cigarettes for them. "The old road they called El Camino Real passed by here and the story goes that when a party of Mexicans was lingerin' here one of the women was dragged right off the land and into the water by one of the creatures and that the spirit of that woman haunts the lake."

"Alligators, eh? I never saw one of those creatures. Maybe we'll be lucky and spot a few."

"I won't swear that there's 'gators in there," said Fisher grimly, "but plenty of human bones would be found if you could drain it, that's for sure." He broke open a mischievous smile. "But what I'd look for if that water ever dried up is . . . silver and gold! Tons of it is down there, according to legend."

"First it's ghosts, now it's silver and gold. C'mon! I know when my leg's being pulled."

Fisher shot up an arm. "On my oath! There's precious metal to be found. It was bein' shipped by wagon train, years back. They made camp by the side of the lake but while they slept, the land sank beneath them, on account of the weight. They was just sucked down and under. Ever since then the Mexicans who live around here tell of a phantom wagon that can be heard rumbling around during the dark of the moon."

"Yeah. Right," scoffed Tyrone.

With a sidelong glance and half a smile, Fisher asked, "You don't believe in ghosts?"

"Shoot no," said Tyrone on a plume of smoke.

"Me neither," laughed Fisher, riding on, "but if there are such things, this lake must be full of spirits that would like to get their hands on my friend Saldana, 'cause this was his favorite spot for dumpin' the bodies of his victims. Must be at least twenty by now."

"Any of yours?"

"I'm a Christian, sir," said King, flipping the stub of his cigar in a long arc toward the lake. "I always gave the men I shot a decent burial. You be sure to put that in whatever you might choose to write about me, hear?"

"I give you my word."

"I'm an honest man, you see. I may have to get tough from time to time, and I know there's folks that look on me as nothin' but a criminal. I don't say I never done wrong. Come Judgment Day I'll have plenty to answer for. But this is a tough land, Tyrone, and toughness is required to tame it. This is a territory that has to be grabbed by the throat. It's not pleasant to witness. But I'm confident that the day will come when the roughnecks like me will be looked back on and judged differently, for the truth is, me and men like me are the ones that are buildin' Texas into a great place."

"Does that go for your pal Saldana?"

Fisher barked a laugh that echoed back from the lake. "Well, I'll tell you the truth about him, too. Sally's about the orn'riest creature I ever ran across. By no stretch of the imagination could you describe Sally as a builder. He's all take and no give. That's the difference between us. And I can say with absolute confidence that if you was to ask him, he'd tell you the exact same thing."

"Maybe one day I'll be able to put the question to him direct."

Fisher stopped his big horse and turned sidewise in the ornate, creaking saddle. "You know, my friend, I believe you would have the gumption to ride into Hezekiah, walk up to Sally, tap him on the shoulder and introduce yourself; just like that, fearless!"

Tyrone shrugged. "What could he do? Gobble me up like one of the alligators in Espantosa Lake?"

Riding on, Fisher laughed. "He just might!"

"Maybe so," said Tyrone, galloping forward, "but I'd be a mighty stringy meal going down."

TWENTY-THREE

Saldana

"Roll out of that sack and saddle up that red pony of yours," blared Fisher, barging into Tyrone's room at dawn the next day. "We've got a long hard road ahead of us."

"A road to where?" said Tyrone, sleepily.

"Why, to Hezekiah, of course!"

Tales of his life poured from Fisher until midafternoon when they reached rugged hill country of lush, deep valleys and windswept, treeless mesas. In the far distance, blue mountains rose against graying skies. "Rough country, ain't it?" said Fisher, admiringly.

"Peaceful," said Tyrone.

"Over thataway lies Uvalde," said Fisher, pointing east. "We'll be at the Nueces soon."

Ten miles up from the meeting of the two branches of the Nueces where the river made a sharp bend and Turkey Mountain loomed ahead of them, they climbed out of a narrow valley. "Not far now," Fisher announced.

For the next hour, the land was hilly and the trail they followed twisting.

Then, abruptly, as they curved around the foot of yet

another steep hill, the trail was blocked by a log gate guarded by a thick-set Mexican squinting down the barrel of a long rifle until he recognized the man in his sights. "It's you, King," he bellowed, lowering the gun and cradling it in the crook of his left elbow. "Long time, no see."

"Evenin' Pablo," said Fisher, riding on as the guard pulled the gate back.

In a valley between steep hillsides, the rising trail widened far enough to accommodate eight horses abreast, Tyrone noted.

It crested half a mile past the gate, revealing an almost square mesa sprinkled with buildings. "Welcome to Hezekiah," declared Fisher.

"Why, it's a regular town," gasped Tyrone.

Spurring Old Yaller forward, Fisher laughed, "Sally likes his creature comforts."

Amazement still flickered in Tyrone's eyes when they pulled up before a rambling log house built on a knoll that afforded a view of the entire settlement.

On the plank porch with his buckskin boots planted wide and his big fists propped on his hips, Saldana stood six and a half feet tall, at least, Tyrone judged. The roof and a yellow straw broad-brimmed floppy sombrero shaded his face from a slant of fading sunlight that revealed a brilliant blue broadcloth coat, orange shirt, red neckerchief and tan riding breeches. "Well ain't you a sight for sore eyes?" he bawled.

Fisher leapt from his horse. "Sally, meet my friend Tyrone. He's a writer who thinks he sees a story in you and me."

"A scribbler, eh?" said Saldana, clomping down from the porch with a wide grin revealing all of his teeth, as sparkling-white as pearls except one in the front which was glinting gold set with a diamond. In the shape of the blade of a Bowie knife, a scar curved from below his right eye to the corner of the broad mouth. His grip was iron and his brown eyes were cold steel and restless, surveying Tyrone's face as steadily and deeply as Tyrone studied the visage of this man who, if Andy Wofford's Book of Knaves had it right, was a ruthless cattle thief, bank robber, murderer and kidnapper of young girls. "Any friend of the King's a friend of mine," he said. *"Mi casa, su casa!"*

TWENTY-FOUR

Table Talk

Like the Mexican desperado, Juan Nepomuceno Cortina who had schooled him, Saldana had the ruddy complexion known as *huero.* A wide forehead hinted of intelligence and stretched above thick, rust-colored eyebrows slanting devil-like toward a hawklike nose which cast a shadow over a drooping mustache bracketing the lips that were quick to smile and reveal the diamond-set gold tooth, but no warmth. Without its livid scar, Tyrone would have described the face as cruel.

"I was born in 1843 at Camargo, Tamaulipas, and was a hellrake as a kid," bragged Saldana, relishing telling his own story over their supper of beefsteak and roasted potatoes. He'd joined the Cortinistas at the age of fourteen, he continued proudly, raiding throughout the Zona Libre and rising in the ranks of Cortina's army of bandits until he killed a man and fled to the sanctuary of his family in Taos and Santa Fe and then to a season of hell-raising with cousins in Tascosa in the rugged Llano Estacado of the Texas panhandle. "But soon I was back along the Rio Grande where Cortina himself gave me permission to organize my own gang. Of course, Cortina had to be paid his tribute."

As he was speaking, the meal was being served wordlessly by a pretty Mexican girl.

Was she the one Saldana had kidnapped? Tyrone wondered.

Soon he had his answer.

"Evangeline!" shouted Saldana angrily. "Our guests need more beef. Bring more beef!"

Like a frightened deer, the girl scampered from the room.

"Juan had to have his *pecho,* which was a kind of tax," continued Saldana. "Out of each herd taken, he had to have every fifth one."

"A twenty percent tax seems pretty steep," said Tyrone as the girl rushed back with a heaping plate of meat.

Saldana shrugged. "If you didn't pay it you would lose everything." Lifting a tableknife, he drew it lightly across his neck. "Understand?"

"Clearly!"

"Don't tell me that such things don't happen in New York City," boomed Saldana. "I've heard about the gangs in New York from men on the ships that put into the seaports on the Gulf coast."

"Like the grass that looks greener in the next fellow's pasture," interjected Fisher, "the gang that's far away seems romantic compared to the nearby, isn't that right, Tyrone? That's why the people of New York prefer to read about the West, hmm?"

"That's one way to see it," answered Tyrone, putting down his fork.

"Done eatin' already?" blurted Saldana incredulously. "There's plenty more where that beef came from!"

"That's my limit," said Tyrone, raising his hands as if in surrender.

"Don't just stand there girl!" snapped Saldana, raising a fist. "Take away the man's plate."

"Thank you," said Tyrone softly, smiling at her as she obeyed. "Are you also the cook? It was a fine meal."

The girl blinked but said nothing.

"The man's talkin' to you, bitch," growled Saldana, jerking her arm. "Answer him or you'll answer to me later."

"N-no, sir, I don't cook," she whispered nervously as she picked up Tyrone's plate, "I just cleans up."

Shoving her aside, Saldana thundered, "Take that out, then bring coffee to us in the parlor whilst we smoke our cee-gars."

TWENTY-FIVE

The Girl

When they finished their coffee, they stepped onto the porch of Saldana's house where a breeze caught the smoke from their cigars, swirling it into eddies and adding its pungent aroma to the tangy smell of the smoke rising from the chimneys of scattered huts while long shadows of dusk fingered their way through Hezekiah. "Snug little retreat, ain't it?" said Saldana proudly.

"Like a fortress," answered Tyrone.

"When I first chanced upon this little valley," confided Saldana, drawing up a chair, "there wasn't but one cabin belongin' to an old trapper, long since departed." He plopped into the chair and cocked back on it, propping his feet against a rail. "I was on the lam from the law, of course, havin' shook off a posse down toward Uvalde." Shifting his cigar from the left to the right side of his mouth, he glanced sidelong at Fisher. "You remember the time, King."

"Plain as yesterday," he replied. Seated on the top step of the porch and leaning against an upright, he chuckled. "I figured you wouldn't stop runnin' till you hit California."

"What I had on my mind was reachin' Santa Fe, but onct I saw this little dent in the mountains, I got the idea that it would make a neat little hideout, so I settled. That summer I collected myself a gang of sorts. Just a handful of men at first. But what I found later was that the word sort of spread and pretty soon other owlhoots and gunslicks started driftin' in until now I got about twenty, all tucked away in their own cabins, as you can see. And fortified so as to persuade any lawmen in the territory not to tread anywheres near the place. If they could find it, that is."

While he was speaking, Evangeline appeared at the corner of the cabin carrying a dishpan of sloshing water on her way to dumping it in tall weeds several yards away.

"I say it again; that's a pretty girl," said Tyrone, standing at the end of the porch watching her.

"Yeah, but she's gotten to be an age where she's more trouble than she's worth," said Saldana grumpily. "There ain't nothin' worse than a female who forgets her place more than she remembers it. The day's comin' when I'll have to send her down."

Tyrone wheeled around. "Send her down?"

"To tend to the men's needs 'stead of to mine," said Saldana. Flipping away the butt of his cigar, he stood and tugged up on his pants. "Let me show you round the town," he said, stepping down to the ground.

It was a town in every sense, with two roads intersecting the main stem, a dozen cabins to house the men, a livery and blacksmith, a general store and a saloon with no name where there were no posted warnings against wearing sidearms.

An instant of silence gripped the one big room when they entered, but there was no way of telling if it was because of Saldana suddenly appearing in the midst of the men, the sight of the legendary King Fisher or the arrival of a stranger.

"So how long you fixin' on stayin', King?" asked

Saldana as they settled at a table at the back of the room, rumbling once more with a dozen baritone voices.

"Headin' back to the Pendencia tomorrow."

"What's your hurry?"

"I got business to attend to. I only came to escort Tyrone. He's capable of findin' his way back when it suits him."

"Maybe he'll like it here and stay," laughed Saldana. "I can always use an extra hand. What about it, Tyrone? Do you think you might be cut out for the life of a bandido? Somethin' tells me that gun you pack has been used for more than target practice. Don't know what it is about you, exactly. The eyes, maybe. They got a certain look to 'em."

"Aw, that's just from the smoke in this place," answered Tyrone, shrugging.

Saldana guffawed and slapped Tyrone's shoulder. "The smoke in this place! I like that! I like you. I think me and you's gonna get along fine!"

The two days following Fisher's departure were a Saldana monologue as they remained indoors in face of the weather turning ugly, starting with twenty-four hours of hard, cold rain that soaked the earth into thick mud which froze at night as the sky cleared, only to cloud-up again, this time bringing snow. But the parlor of Saldana's cabin was snug, warmed by a roaring wood fire in a potbelly stove tended to slavishly by Evangeline while Saldana spun out his bloody history.

She never spoke except when spoken to, quaking with fear at every reproach from Saldana's mouth. But her eyes, Tyrone thought, conveyed what she might have said had she the courage to do so—fear and loathing and hatred for Saldana but, he believed, curiosity and possibly warmth toward himself.

She really was quite pretty, he thought, but could have

been even more attractive were she permitted to fix herself up with a proper hairdo and a fancy dress instead of tying her long brown hair into a knot and wearing a plain brown cotton dress with an apron.

He wondered how her laughter would sound. A giggle? The clear ringing of a bell? Or deep and throaty, like Peggy Doyle's chesty laughing amidst the rowdiness of the Garden of Eden back in New York so long ago it seemed a lifetime?

His stolen glances at the girl did not go unnoticed. "You seem to have an eye for that stuff," declared Saldana on the third day after Fisher's leaving. "Did you ever have yourself a Mexican wench?"

"No, I never did," said Tyrone, apprehensively.

Saldana snorted. "Well, be careful, 'cause that one's got claws!"

A puzzling remark, it nagged Tyrone later when he sat inscribing notes of Saldana's endless dissertation upon the subject of his life. Hunched forward into a pool of light from an oil lamp, he worked beneath a window at a table in a small cabin which Saldana had had vacated of its usual occupant for his use, pausing now and then to ponder a delicate way to phrase some Saldana atrocity or simply to listen to the wind rattling the panes and whistling through cracks in the log walls.

In his notebook he also sketched the layout of Hezekiah, carefully placing all the buildings and noting their use, all with the intention of fixing the details on paper rather than having to rely on memory if he ever did decide to turn the lives of King Fisher and Saldana into a book to thrill and chill Eastern readers. But the crude drawing, he realized, could serve as well as a map for Andy Wofford's Rangers should they ever undertake to raid the hideout.

And what about all that he had written down of Saldana's recitation of a string of heinous crimes? Might a court of law accept them as a confession?

Might Saldana hang because of my notebooks? he wondered as a coyote wailed balefully in the far distance.

Fully dressed save for his boots, he lay on the bed, curling up beneath a pair of coarse blankets and facing the stove that was struggling to provide warmth in a night that grew progressively wilder, filled with the whistle of the wind, shaking windows and the plaintive call of the coyote that together began to lull him to sleep.

Then a blast of cold woke him, the quick opening and closing of the door.

Leaning against it, hugging herself in a shawl, Evangeline whispered, "Saldana sent me to you."

TWENTY-SIX

Escaping the Beast

Tyrone bolted up, rubbing his eyes, not knowing how long he'd been asleep.

Chilling fear sliced through him.

Had Saldana discovered the truth about him? Somehow, did this spider who lurked at the center of a web of criminals feel the flutter of a strand reaching all the way back to Wichita? Had someone arrived at Hezekiah during the night and, hearing the name Tyrone, remembered it as belonging to the man who'd killed Moe Ludlum? Might someone else have seen him in the company of Andy Wofford? Was the truth about him known? Would he be branded a spy and meted out a spy's penalty? Had this winsome, frightened, trembling girl been sent to summon him to his own hanging?

Or had King Fisher really discerned everything from the start and brought him here to be dealt with in secret by his murderous old friend?

"What is it, Evangeline? Trouble?"

"No trouble," she whispered, shaking her head slowly.

Relieved, he almost laughed. "If you've come to see about the fire, Evangeline, it's fine."

"No," she said, "I have not come for that."

He studied her shadowed beauty. "Then what is it that brings a pretty girl out on a night like this?"

Hesitantly, she answered, "Saldana sent me to . . . stay . . . with you. 'Go warm the bed of our visitor,' he said."

The words hit Tyrone like a slap. "That's outrageous! No, I won't allow it. That son of a bitch!"

Rushing to him, she begged, "Please, please, it's all right." Her arms circled him tightly. "Don't make trouble."

"Look, Evangeline, I'm not going to stand for . . ."

"He's drunk. Crazy drunk," she pleaded. "If you argue with him it will not be good. He'll take offense."

"Too damned bad," he said, peeling away her tight embrace.

Clutching his hand, she cried, "No, please. I do not mind, truly. It's best this way. I don't want you to be killed."

"It's him who's likely to be killed."

"If you kill him, his men will then kill you. I do not want you killed because of me."

"No, of course not," he said quietly as he folded her gently into his arms, "but the cruel bastard deserves a little killing. Where does he get off pulling such a stunt, sending you here without even asking me if I was interested."

She jerked away and studied him with hurting eyes. "You don't care for me?"

"Oh, geez, I didn't mean it that way! Why, you're a damned pretty girl. I have to admit I've had a hard time keeping my eyes off you. I suppose Saldana couldn't help noticing it—but by Christ, that doesn't give him the right to force you to sleep with me. You're a human being, not chattel. We just had a war to settle the issue of slavery!"

"With you I wouldn't feel like a slave," she said, speaking so softly he could barely hear her above the howl of the wind. "I confess that I have been looking at you, too.

At first I thought you were one more of his outlaw friends. But I noticed right away that you seemed different. You talked nice to me. You didn't boss me around or cuss at me the way others do. And you didn't eat like a pig at a trough, either."

"If my mama taught me anything," he laughed, hugging her tightly, "it was how to behave at the supper table. There wasn't a lot to eat on that table most of the time, but what there was got devoured decently. If I didn't mind my manners, I got a right smart slap from mama." Releasing her, he examined her face. "Does he slap you?"

She averted ashamed eyes. "Sometimes."

"Beats you?"

"Yes," she sobbed.

"The dirty skunk bastard! Why do you stay with him? Why haven't you run away?"

She moved to the window, gazing out at the wild night. "I don't know the way out of here. I don't even know where I am, Texas or Mexico."

"Texas," he answered gently, striding to her. "Up near Turkey Mountain on the Nueces, west of Uvalde." He embraced her. "Now you know."

Bursting into tears, she buried her face in his shoulder. "It doesn't matter where I am. He would track me down."

"Can you ride a horse?" he asked, pushing her to arms' length.

"Yes, but . . ."

"Never mind the buts," he asserted, spinning away from her and hurriedly collecting his things. "Tell me about the stable. Does anybody watch it at night?"

"No. There's no need."

"That's good," he said, stuffing his possessions into a saddle bag, " 'cause I'd sure like to get us outta here without having to shoot my way out."

"Oh no, please," she gasped, shrinking back from him. "It's much too risky."

"You let me worry about the risk, darlin'," he said,

opening the door a crack. Surveying the space between the cabin and the livery at the far end of the street, he found the huts of the men dark and the road lifeless. The fierce sky which had brought the rain was turgid with scudding, ripped gray clouds that alternately hid and revealed a three-quarter moon which lit Hezekiah brightly one minute and darkened it the next.

By moving in the patches of dark, he explained to the girl, and with luck, they could reach the stable, get Redskin and a horse for her and be long gone before anybody noticed their absence. "Ready to go for it?" he asked.

"I'm so scared," she sobbed.

"That's two of us," he answered, gripping her cold hand tightly. "C'mon!"

Crouching low, they darted into shielding brush.

Pressed against him, she was trembling, though whether it was from her fright or the cold he couldn't say.

Probably both, he thought.

To their right, Saldana's big house was an immense shadow, like a large, black, sleeping beast.

Creeping, he led her in silver light to the left, waited for the clouds to cover the moon and scampered to the cover of the rear of the first of the men's cabins where even through thick log walls he could hear their rasping snores. Again they dashed, waited for the moon to be hidden, and dashed again until they came to a broad stretch of moonwashed, waist-high grass between the last of the huts and the stable. Beyond the livery, the road twisted toward the gate that had been guarded on the day he'd arrived. Would there be a man there now? he wondered as, anxiously, he waited for clouds to slide over the moon once more, praying that it would remain dark enough long enough to cover a final dash to the stable.

With the chill wind at their backs, they waited in a silence broken only by the familiar neighing of a horse in the barn. Worrying that Redskin might have picked up their scent, he could only hope that he and the other animals would not create a racket and alert Saldana and his sleeping henchmen. Would there be a man posted in the barn? he wondered, scanning the ragged clouds for any sign of one to blot out the moon.

Lying in the wet grass, they waited minutes before the light dimmed.

"Keep down and crawl," he whispered. "Stay close to me."

Unguarded, the stable doors were wide open.

Just inside, an oil lamp hung from a nail.

Trembling, Evangeline held it while Tyrone struck a match.

Its flare gave her face the look of an elegant painting but cast an eerie glow that threw giant shadows of the horses against the walls.

Redskin's stall was the third on the right. "Easy fella," Tyrone whispered, stroking its nose. "Don't give us away, boy." Next to Redskin was a blocky gray. Both were haltered. "Thanks be for small favors," Tyrone whispered. "Lead 'em out and up the road," he said to the girl. "I'll fetch the rest of the rigging and a couple of saddles."

The sky was nearly clear when he caught up with her but the light-giving moon was at a low enough angle above the hillside to create shielding shadows at the left of the road.

Now for that damned gate, Tyrone thought as they walked the horses away from Hezekiah. Please let it be unattended, he said to himself. They'd been damned lucky so far, he thought; let it hold a little longer. But fifty yards farther, the luck ran out in the form of a sentry leaning against the gate's upright. Long and lanky and looking bored as he smoked a cigarette, he was in tan buckskins from hat to boots except for the slanted slash of a black gunbelt supporting a Colt Patterson in a black holster cinched to his right thigh, and a sheathed Bowie knife on his left hip.

"It is Mendoza," Evangeline whispered. "I hate him. Shoot him!"

"Can't shoot him," answered Tyrone. "A shot'd bring the whole bunch at a run."

Pondering this for a moment, she stared at the guard through slitted, hateful eyes. "Do you have a knife? I will cut his throat. I loathe him."

"Sorry, no knife," he said. "Why do you hate him?"

"The way he looks at me all the time," she said with disgust. "He undresses me with his eyes. Only a fear of Saldana has kept him from trying something."

"What do you think he'd do if you were to walk up to him right now? Suppose you went up to him as if you'd come to give him what he wants? Could you keep him busy thinking about you while I . . ."

Her narrowed eyes opened wide. "Ah, I get it! While he is looking at me, you sneak around and . . ."

"I come at him from behind and put him out of business. You willing to give it a try?"

"You'll kill him?"

"No, just coldcock him with the butt of my gun."

"Very well," she said, sounding disappointed.

"Good. Give me a headstart. Count to fifty. Slow. Then walk up to him, making sure he faces the other side of the road."

"Don't worry," she said, jutting out her chin. "I know what to do."

Like a crab on Shanghai Pierce's beach, he crept sidewise through the brush of the dark side of the hill, keeping his eyes on the broad road bathed in moonlight until, as brazen as brass, Evangeline appeared from the shadows. Lightfooted and confident, she looked like a schoolgirl prancing gaily out to a picnic. Startled, the guard came upright. "Evening, Mendoza," she said quietly as she neared.

"Well if it ain't you," he said eagerly, flipping away his cigarette. "What's this all about?"

Close enough to stroke his face, she did so. "Whatcha think it's about, honey?"

"Does the boss know you're here?" Mendoza asked, his voice as fragile as glass.

"He's passed out drunk."

As her delicate hand drifted down to Mendoza's chest, Tyrone eased from the covering brush.

"I was lonely," she whispered, circling Mendoza's narrow hips with her arms, "and I got to thinkin' about you out here all by yourself."

Catfooting across the road, Tyrone slid out his Colt and held it by the ice-cold barrel.

"Are you crazy?" gasped Mendoza. "If the boss finds out he'll string us both up."

"You should kill him," she said. "You're the one who should be boss of Hezekiah." Her right hand dropped to his Bowie knife. "Cut his throat while he sleeps," she said throatily. "With this," she said, pulling out the big, heavy knife.

The blade of the Bowie flashed moonlight as Tyrone raised the Colt over Mendoza's head then brought it down hard.

"Uhn," grunted Mendoza.

As his eyes rolled back, he buckled at the knees and arched backward, slamming against Tyrone and sliding into a crumpled heap at his feet.

Tyrone jerked back.

Mendoza flopped over.

Evangeline lunged, plunging the knife into his chest.

"Die, pig," she cried, stabbing him repeatedly.

Seizing her flailing arm, Tyrone grunted, "Enough, enough."

TWENTY-SEVEN

The Good and the Bad

"We'll keep to the river," said Tyrone urgently, "and hope that they won't be able to track us."

Evangeline's answer was a quick nod of her head.

The moonlight through gaps in trees dappled the Nueces, running swiftly now after the rain and adding its rushing roar to the sound-filled night and the sloshing of their horses' hooves.

"Maybe we should head for Uvalde," he said. "We can rest up there."

"No," she said sharply. "Saldana has many friends there."

"We're gonna have to stop somewhere to eat and rest. And let's face it, you're not exactly dressed for riding."

"Do not worry about me. When it is daylight I will leave you and go to San Antonio. I have relatives there."

"I can't let you do that by yourself," he protested. "A girl traveling alone in this country? No."

"I am not a girl," she snapped. "I was before Saldana took me. I am a woman now."

The memory of her stabbing Mendoza flashed in his head. "Yeah, I guess you are," he said.

"It's you who will have to be careful," she said. "You're the one Saldana will fear. You know too much."

She was right, of course, he thought. Amazingly, Saldana had poured out his entire life and what he'd said had been written down. What was contained in the notebooks in his saddlebags was a recitation of a string of outrageous crimes that a court of law might accept as a confession. Hadn't Saldana grasped the possibility that his rambling, prideful and boasting discourse upon his outlawing might be turned against him and lead to his hanging? If Wofford and McNelly got their hands on the pages, they surely would use them, he thought as they plodded down the snaking river, and undoubtedly they would want him to testify as to their veracity.

Like a knife point, the possibility that because of his written words Saldana might go to the gallows stabbed into him. Did he want that? Was it his duty to see Saldana hanged? Or was it none of his business, really? He'd come west to gather stories for the firm of Beadle and Adams to publish in their cheap little thrillers, not to be an arm of the law. Wasn't there supposed to be a line between men like him and Wofford? Was it right for him to get involved with the people he'd been hired to write about? Back in New York, Mulberry Street had been that line; the cops on one side, the reporters on the other.

Out here in the West, there were no lines, no fences, no clear-cut distinctions, either on the land or between the people.

King Fisher was evidence of that. To a lawman like Wofford he was a criminal, yet to the men and women of Eagle Pass and the Nueces Strip he was as much the hero as the knave.

This was a rough country, Fisher had said. Today's outlaw became tomorrow's civic leader. Tomorrow's hero.

Rebecca Colter had made the same point. Texas was a

land that had to be grabbed by the throat and tamed, she'd said.

He remembered the salesman on the train going to Wichita and his glowing admiration for the James brothers. In Hicks' mind, the Jameses weren't outlaws but daring poor boys who had the guts to do what every American would like to do.

Morgan came to mind. The Gun Man of Abilene! And Charlie Carew's animated telling of Morgan's exploits with a Colt pistol that had made Morgan famous all over Kansas.

And King Fisher? To the Texas Rangers he may have become a knave, but to most of the people of the Nueces Strip, wasn't he a hero?

What was it in the character of Americans that drove them to embrace bad men and drape them in godlike myth? he wondered as he guided Redskin along the edge of the Nueces and hoped they were leaving no trail for Saldana to follow.

They'd been riding for more than an hour when they reached the confluence of the branches of the Nueces while the first glimmerings of yellow dawn broke through the trees. "Probably they have not yet missed us," suggested Evangeline as they paused to let the horses water. "When the men drink at night they sleep late," she said, peering anxiously at the sky. "With the sun up they will discover Mendoza. Then they will come after us. No matter how long it takes, Saldana will search for us. He does not forgive. By helping me, you've made an enemy for life. Why did you do it?"

"I guess I'm just a sucker for a woman in trouble," he answered light-heartedly, thinking back to the Garden of Eden and his rising to the defense of an aging whore, forging the first link in the amazing chain of events that had brought him in the company of a willful Mexican woman to a fork in a river in the heart of a wilderness in Texas.

"This is where I'll leave you," she declared, shaking her long brown hair. "We must not continue together. We must not give them one trail. San Antonio is straight east. We could meet there later."

"Maybe we will."

"Which way do you go now?"

"South. To Carrizo Springs."

"Go carefully there. That's King Fisher's country. He will soon hear about what has happened."

"Believe me," he grunted as Redskin lifted his head, his thirst slaked. "I have no intention of looking him up."

Abruptly, she leaned toward him and kissed him. *"Vaya con dios."*

Climbing from the river bank, he paralleled it, keeping its valley on his left to the east and low mountains to the west, letting Redskin set the pace until early afternoon when they crossed a rise and he discovered the sparkle of the sun upon Espantosa Lake.

Midway between the lake and Carrizo Springs, Wofford's bivouac was an oasis in the form of a circle of tents in a tree-shaded hollow with a waterhole at the center. Thirty men selected by Wofford in San Antonio, they'd been camped for a week, each armed with a brand-new Winchester and a satchel of ammunition paid for by Shanghai Pierce. "I'd like to be ridin' with you when you clean out that Saldana gang," he'd said with booming enthusiasm, "but since Captain McNelly's ruled it out, sayin', quite rightly, that this is a young man's mission, I can at least see to it that your men have the best there is in firepower."

Whether the guns would be used would depend on what Tyrone could find out concerning Saldana's whereabouts, Wofford pointed out. "We picked up information in Eagle Pass that he made contact with Fisher and that the two of them seemed to hit it off. But whether Fisher will be willin' to lead Tyrone to Saldana is a question. And even if that happens there's no tellin' how long it might be till we get word from Tyrone. It's all a big gamble."

"Don't you worry about Tyrone," answered Shanghai confidently. "He'll come through for you. He's a good man."

A perimeter rider was the first to see him. Spotted through field glasses as he turned the eastern edge of the lake at a gallop, he fit the description Wofford had provided of him and his horse. "Approach anyone who fits," Wofford had ordered. "Identify yourself as belonging to Wofford's Rangers. If it's Tyrone, he'll take it from there." Expectantly, the Ranger sped toward the lake, a distance of two miles.

Tyrone saw the dust trail before he spotted the lone rider rushing toward him. "Well, well, what have we here?" he said to Redskin. He rested a cautious hand on his gun. "Friend or foe?"

"Howdy," said the rider as he drew up. "The name's Gordon. Texas Rangers, Lieutenant Wofford in command."

Relieved, Tyrone lifted his hand from his gun. "I'm Tyrone!"

"Well, I'm pleased to hear it," grinned the Ranger, snapping a hand to the brim of his black hat in a smart salute. "You're just the man the lieutenant's been waitin' for!"

"Eat now," said Wofford curtly as the cook set a plate of beef and beans before Tyrone, seated at a folding table in Wofford's tent. "When you're done, you can make your report on the Saldana gang."

"I'll eat *and* report," insisted Tyrone, scooping beans

onto a slice of bread. "The sooner I give it to you, the sooner you can get your men up to Hezekiah and clean out the cursed place."

"Well it won't be today, so take your time. No use splittin' a gut."

"Why not today?" demanded Tyrone indignantly, glaring across the table.

"First off, you need some rest," barked Wofford, rocking back in his chair. "You look a wreck, frankly. Second, the movement of thirty Rangers will take some planning. Third, it'll have to be timed so's to get us there at the crack of dawn. Wherever there is."

"Fifty miles north and west as the crow flies," said Tyrone, spearing a chunk of blood-red beefsteak. "There's a little valley on this side of the Nueces at the foot of Turkey Mountain."

"Way up there?" said Wofford, standing. "I always figured he'd be holed up somewhere along the Rio Grande," he said, pacing. "Maybe even over on the Mexican side."

"He probably figured you'd figure it that way," said Tyrone, smiling mischievously. "The man's a thug and probably insane, but he's not dumb." Chewing, he added, "I've got a map of the layout of Hezekiah in my saddle bag."

Wofford sat. "How many men's he got?"

"A dozen, give or take one or two, when I skeedaddled last night. Some of 'em, maybe all, may be out looking for me and the girl."

Wofford jerked back. "What girl?"

"The one Saldana will soon regret he ever beat up," said Tyrone, reaching for a cup of coffee. "You wouldn't happen to have some Irish whiskey to lace this with? I always seem to talk better when I've got some Irish behind my belt."

"Sorry. Rye's the Rangers' drink."

"That'll do."

Wofford left the table and rummaged in his saddle bags, producing a full flask.

By the time Tyrone was finished making his report concerning Saldana, Hezekiah and Evangeline's knifing of Mendoza, it was empty and Wofford was staring at him with amazement. "Jesus, she must be some piece of work. I'd sure like to have her give testimony at Saldana's trial."

A sly smile creased the corners of Tyrone's mouth. "Oh, is there going to be a trial?"

TWENTY-EIGHT

Return to Hezekiah

Two days later in the last light of a setting full moon, Wofford's Rangers single-filed up from the Nueces and moved westward through hoof-muffling dewy grass as high as the horses' knees.

When they reached the last turn before coming to the gate that guarded the road to Hezekiah, a pinkish dawn was beginning to spill across the ridges of thin washboard clouds. "Now let's see about that gate," whispered Wofford, sliding off a savvy blocky bay that stood as still as a statue.

Redskin pranced a bit but made no noise as Tyrone stepped down to catfoot behind Wofford to a shielding mesquite thicket with a clear view of the gate.

A lone figure paced slowly behind it.

"Just the one," whispered Wofford. "That's good. I was afraid there'd be more. Ranger Donnelly will pick him off neat and clean."

A minute later, ruddy-faced, freckled and rusty-haired, Patrick Donnelly, who'd served in the war as a sniper with Shelby, eased into the mesquite thicket, wet the sights of his shiny new Winchester, followed the sentry until he was out of the road and fired one shot that sounded like a sneeze. It drilled the sentry through the head.

Immediately, a lone Ranger galloped to the gate and lifted it clear of the road.

Four abreast, Wofford's Rangers raced past the gate and quickly up the hill toward Hezekiah.

"You stay with me for now, Tyrone," ordered Wofford, grabbing Redskin's reins and pulling him to a halt as the Rangers rode past. "I need you alive to identify Saldana."

From the crest of the hill, Tyrone looked down on Saldana's little village. As the Rangers poured up the street, orange flames of gunfire spit from the windows and doors of the cabins like the tongues of snakes as Saldana's men opened fire, answered by volleys from the Rangers' pistols and Winchester rifles that were like fierce hail splintering wood and shattering glass.

Wrenched from their sleep, startled and confused, others had rushed outside and were shooting wildly at the first rank of Rangers they encountered only to be cut down by the next as Wofford's men surged forward in the direction of Saldana's cabin at the top of the sloping street.

Rifle fire keenly aimed from the cabin was deadly, dropping three of the six nearest riders.

Leaping from their horses, the others sought cover behind a water trough, opening up with Winchesters and peppering the front of the cabin.

Having swept up the street, the Rangers wheeled round and thundered back, guns blazing and raking the buildings, but when they turned again, several dismounted.

Crouching, they dashed past the livery and through the same high grass that Tyrone and Evangeline had used to cover their escape as those on horseback drenched the windows of the nearest cabins with rifle fire. Crawling, they reached the sides of the nearest cabins.

The covering firing stopped.

"Gonna smoke 'em out," said Wofford, pointing. "Each of those men has a leather pouch filled with rags soaked in coal oil. They pull out a little shirttail of rag, light it with a match and chuck the whole bundle through a window. It'll make more fear than fire and plenty of smoke. And if that doesn't chase 'em out, the men will torch those thatched rooftops. That'll bring 'em into the daylight, sure. Oh what I'd give to have an artillery piece!"

As he spoke, the men who had been raining covering fire on the cabins charged forward again, pounding up the street, firing into buildings as they proceeded, turned again, raced back and turned once more.

"By God, they are magnificent," cried Wofford. "What about those men, Tyrone? Aren't they just goddamned glorious?"

When it was finished, three of the Rangers had been killed and five wounded.

Twelve of the Saldana gang were dead and six severely wounded. Only two surrendered unscathed.

Acrid gunsmoke mixing with the smoldering of cabins that had been set afire and the wood-smelling flow from chimneys of unscorched huts hung like a thick fog above the town as Tyrone and Wofford dismounted and strode from body to body looking for Saldana. "Nope," said Tyrone, glancing at each lifeless face until they were standing in front of Saldana's cabin with no corpse unseen. "He's not here," Tyrone said, his voice shrill with pain and anger. "The son of a bitch wasn't even here."

"He was here," said Wofford forcefully.

Turning sharply, he marched toward the rear of the cabin.

Dashing after him, Tyrone found him kneeling and fingering churned earth below an open door. "See? A man's boots where he mounted. He's ridin' a big horse. And look at this hoofprint. The right hind. See there? One of the nails is missin'. Thank God for small favors. That missin' nail's gonna make trackin' a whole lot easier. The trail goes that way." He pointed to the west. "There must be another way out of this hollow in that direction," he said, rising. "Well, he can run but he sure as hell can't do it without leavin' a trail marked by that blessed tattletale missin' nail. Where that trail leads, I follow." He glanced sidelong at Tyrone. "You comin'?"

"Try and stop me."

"Good man," grunted Wofford. Turning sharply, he barked orders to Ranger Donnelly. See to the wounded. Bury the dead. Deliver the captured pair and the wounded to the jail in Uvalde. Confiscate the horses and any other property worth having. Burn Hezekiah to the ground. Then proceed to San Antonio to report to Rangers headquarters for further orders.

Seated at a big table in Saldana's parlor, he wrote out a message for McNelly:

> Dear Capn. McNelly,
> The Saldana gang is destroyed and their hideout burnt to the ground. Rangers wounded in this action: 5, not seriously. We suffered 3 dead. Theirs: 12 dead, 6 damaged, 2 alive and being sent to Uvalde. Sorry to report Saldana escaped. I believe may be heading north, so I will pursue with intentions of overtaking and arresting him. As this is a job best done alone, my detachment of Rangers is being sent to you for further orders.

He looked up at Tyrone. "I guess I'd better mention you in here, hunh? The captain took a likin' to you and I wouldn't want to worry him. Don't know how he'll take to the idea of you accompanyin' me, though. He could order me not to. You are a civilian, after all!"

"That's an order he'd have to deliver personally," answered Tyrone, hard as flint. "And then I'd have to tell him where to stuff it, citing my rights in the First Amendment to the Constitution of the United States, which guarantees the freedom of the press, even in Texas!"

With a laugh, Wofford wrote:

> Mr. Tyrone insists on going along with me, so just to make sure it's legal I'll be swearing him in as a Ranger.
>
> Respectfully,
> Lt. A. Wofford

Looking up with a grin, he said, "Consider yourself sworn." Looking down at the badge pinned to his coat, he said, "When all this is done, I'll provide you one of these." A brass star cut within a circle, it bore two words—"Texas" on the star, "Ranger" in the arc below. "It'll be a souvenir," he said, polishing the badge with his sleeve, "unless, of course, you decide to wear it permanently."

TWENTY-NINE

Llano Estacado

The trail of Saldana's distinctive hoofprints ended abruptly at midday on the north side of the Nueces at the edge of a sun-baked field of rock as flat as a table.

"Now what?" said Tyrone dejectedly. "There's no way we're going to track him over a bed of stone."

"Don't fret, *amigo,*" said Wofford, squinting into the glare off the sheetrock. "I've got a pretty good idea where he's headin'." He paused, flicking his tongue to wet his lips. "He's makin' straight north for the Llano Estacado; that's 'Staked Plains' in English. He'll be headin' for a spot west of the Palo Duro Canyon name of Tascosa. He's done it before. He's got cousins there. From Tascosa he may strike west, over to New Mexico and Santa Fe where he's also got family. It's a long haul to Tascosa; five hundred miles at least. He'll be movin' fast, makin' what the Mexicans call a *jornado,* meanin' a full day's travel, sunup to sundown, up to a hundred miles at a clip. If he keeps a *jornado* pace, he'll make Tascosa in six or seven days. That means we have to push ourselves, else he'll slip out of Texas into New Mexico, out of my jurisdiction. Can't have that, can we? You still game?"

"Hell yes!"

"We'll need provisions. We can pick 'em up at Rocksprings."

Climbing constantly into what a map in Wofford's saddlebag declared to be the Edwards Plateau, they pressed their horses hard through a folded landscape fed by creeks and springs and slashed by the valleys of many of the rivers of Texas—the Llano, Medina, Frio, Concho, Pedernales—and rutted with picturesque canyons in limestone hills.

Tucked in the middle of the plateau fifty miles north of Saldana's hideout, Rocksprings was reached just before dusk. Their arrival at Ruderman's general store provided an unexpected boost in the fortunes of the lanky, easygoing proprietor, Sidney, and his pert wife, Elaine, who proved speedy and efficient in gathering their provisions from shelves and bins.

Had they noticed any strangers passing through town that day? Wofford asked. "Other than the two of us, of course!"

"Big man, big horse, gold tooth," added Tyrone urgently.

"A horse with a gold tooth?" asked Sidney, chuckling and rubbing his jaw.

"The man, of course, not the horse," grinned Wofford.

"No such person called on us today," said Elaine, collecting canned goods.

"But that's not to say the fellow didn't pass through town," added Sidney. "Many travel through Rocksprings but few linger. Now, if you gentlemen are interested in spending the night, we've got a comfortable room to let. And the wife's as fine a cook as you'll meet in these parts."

"Temptin' as that sounds," said Wofford, gathering their purchases, "we'll be movin' on, too." Two hours of good daylight remained, he reckoned.

At sundown they had passed the two forks of the Llano and half the distance to San Angelo and were camped beside a small tributary of the river. "From here we'll cut northwest along the Concho to Big Spring, resting ourselves and the horses as little as possible," explained Wofford, unfolding his map and tracing the route with a finger in the flickering light of their campfire. "Saldana's not likely to pause much," he said. "He's smart enough to assume that somebody's after him, so he'll be livin' off the land and his fat, determined to reach the warm embrace of his nefarious kinfolk. It's a curious fact about men who are on the run from the law that they rush back to their homes, as if that's not where they'll be looked for first." He paused thoughtfully, frowning into the fire. "Of course, I could be dead wrong! Maybe Saldana doubled-back and lit into Mexico. Maybe he skeedaddled into the welcoming arms of his old buddy Fisher. Maybe you and I are engaged in the biggest wild goose chase in the history of the Lone Star State!"

"I don't think so," answered Tyrone softly, dipping fingers into his shirt pocket to fish out the makings of two cigarettes.

"Rollin' your own now, eh?" said Wofford. "Now there's a sign that you're well on your way to becomin' a true Texan!"

"I thought a man had to be born here to be true," answered Tyrone teasingly as he passed a ragged cigarette to Wofford and started in on the second.

"After your service to the state in pinpointin' the location of Hezekiah, I think you've earned the privilege. In fact, I think I'll ask Governor Coke to issue a proclamation!"

"Well first off," said Tyrone, lighting up his cigarette with a twig from the fire, "let's make sure we put Saldana out of commission—the low-down son of a bitch."

"Say, you've really turned this thing personal, haven't you?"

"I've got strong feelings about men who beat up on women." He thought of Crazy Sid and Peggy Doyle. And the terror in Evangeline's eyes. And he remembered his mother being beaten by his father. "I guess I always have."

Four days from Hezekiah under slate gray skies and whipped by a cold but dry west wind, they reached an escarpment and climbed it with difficulty, picking their way along a slippery rubble-strewn trail with sheer rising rock cliffs to one side and abrupt fall-offs to the other, but presently, they reached the top and leveled out.

"Jesus," gasped Tyrone. Before him from horizon to horizon stretched a flat but restless sea of grass. "What a place!"

"Welcome to the Llano Estacado," said Wofford. "The Staked Plains of Texas; as challenging a piece of land as you can find."

"Looks harmless," said Tyrone, puzzled.

"Looks are deceivin'," said Wofford as his horse waded into grass that rose to its withers, parted and straightened up and closed as he passed, leaving no sign that anyone had trespassed. "We've seen the last of water for a while."

Forbidding. Daunting. Worthless. Desert. A death trap for the unwary. Useless. These were the words with which these high plains had been described. There was no shade. No potable water. So-called streams were frequently dried-up gullies or quicksand bogs. A man could travel for hundreds of miles and see no vegetation growing taller than sagebrush and prickly shrubs. Its animals were buffalo, antelope, jackrabbits, prairie dogs, toads and rattlesnakes.

Here, in search of the Seven Cities of Gold but finding neither cities, nor gold, nor silver nor anything else worth lingering for, the Spanish conquistador Francisco Vasquez de Coronado had crossed and departed, leaving behind a few spirited horses that were to become the ancestors of herds of fleet-footed mustangs that provided the opportunity for a fierce tribe of Indians to range down from the western mountains and become hunters on horseback, preying on the buffalo, and, when white men moved westward, attacking them; the dreaded Comanches.

"On June 8, 1844, a party of seventy of the Comanche attacked fourteen Texas Rangers along the Pedernales," said Wofford as they pushed north in an arrow-straight line pointing toward Lubbock under an unrelentingly bright but warmthless winter sun. "There were fourteen Rangers, led by John C. Hays, and the savages naturally expected to wipe 'em out. But the Rangers that day had somethin' with them that the redskins had never come up against before, somethin' that changed the whole history of the frontier."

"Namely?" said Tyrone.

"Each of Hays's Rangers carried one of Mr. Samuel Colt's repeating, six-shot pistols, as modified at the suggestion of Samuel H. Walker, a captain of the Rangers. Well, those Colt Walkers extracted a toll of thirty Comanches that day. Of course, cleanin' out the Comanches is primarily an army job now, but I like to think it was the Rangers at the Pedernales that day that marked the beginnin' of the end of the Comanches. When that's finally accomplished, this territory will be safe and, I think, you'll see people floodin' into the Staked Plains and openin' it up to cattle ranchin'. I may do so myself one day, should I ever decide to settle down! That is, if any woman will have what will be a saddle-sore old Texas Ranger by then."

"Why, I suppose any woman would find you a prize catch," teased Tyrone. "At any time and anywhere!"

"I dunno," said Wofford, squinting against the glare of the midday sun. "Texas is a dandy place for men and dogs but hell on horses and women."

THIRTY

The Canyon

In pale yellow twilight on the fifth day since they'd left Hezekiah, they reached the rimrock of the south bluffs of the Prairie Dog Town Fork of the Red River. "We'll make a stop here," declared Wofford, shifting in his saddle and scrutinizing a map propped against the horn. "We're about fifty miles southeast of Amarillo, some seventy from Tascosa. We'll camp down there."

This was Palo Duro Canyon, a gash nearly a thousand feet deep and sixty miles long and varying in width from a few hundred yards to fifteen miles, the only feature of its kind in the High Plains. Deep in its belly, the stream flowing southeast to contribute its waters to the great Red River was banked by a grass-rich valley and lush with cedar, chinaberry and cottonwood.

An old Comanche trail snaked down to it.

"The town of Canyon's nearby, if you can call a trading post and saloon a town," said Wofford as they made camp by the river. "It's one of Saldana's old stomping grounds, so we have to assume that he'll have put out the word to his old buddies to keep a sharp eye peeled for strangers passin' through."

Tethering Redskin at the water's edge, Tyrone looked up. "You really think Saldana knows somebody's chasing him?"

Wofford's eyes narrowed to slits and searched the tops of the high bluffs. "He knows, all right! The bastard could be watching us at this very minute. He's as sly as a fox and subtle as a snake. The closer we've come to this place the more I've thought I felt his eyes on us. Once in a while I even imagined I could smell him!"

Their meal was the last of the provisions bought at Rocksprings, a place far away in time and miles.

"This land will be fine ranchin' country once it's made safe for whites to settle, once it's cleared of the Comanches," said Wofford, finishing a plate of beans. "But that's a job for the army."

"Aw, a lone Ranger could handle it," jibed Tyrone.

Wofford carried his plate to the river for washing. "You think that's a joke," he said, "but let me tell you about the time a sheriff had a riot on his hands and sent up a distress signal, askin' for the help of the Rangers. Well, one Ranger showed up. 'Where's the rest of them?' the sheriff demanded. The Ranger reared back and answered, 'You said you only had one riot!' "

The word that fit Lieutenant Andrew Wofford of the Texas Rangers, Tyrone decided in the quiet of their camp deep in the narrow valley of the Prairie Dog Town Fork of the Red River that night, was 'tenacious.' If he ever wrote a book about Wofford, he decided, that word had to go into the title.

He pictured the book's cover:

WOFFORD OF THE RANGERS
Tenacious Tracker
of the Llano Estacado

"When we find Saldana," he asked, noting that he'd said 'when' not 'if,' a tribute to tenaciousness, "how do you plan to take him?"

"I reckon that'll be up to him," said Wofford, hunkering by the fire to light a cigarette.

"You planning on killing him?"

"I'd hate to have to do that," puffed Wofford, lying back. "A proper hangin's what the people deserve. Plus, a hangin's a lesson to others. Stringin' Saldana up will leave no doubt that one of the worst characters in the Book of Knaves got his just desserts." He held the cigarette out, as if studying it. "If I have to leave him planted in the Staked Plains it won't be easy to get folks to believe that he's really dead. When it comes to assertin' the rule of law, nothin's quite so convincin' as a hanged outlaw on display. 'Course, if I have to kill him, I've got you as a witness." He sat up, grinning. "You can put it in a book! Everyone believes somethin' if it's printed in a book."

"So executing Saldana's not enough! The people have to know about it?"

"That's the way I see it, anyways."

"I know a newspaperman up in Wichita who holds that a public hanging's nothing but an invitation to crooks to lift the wallets of the people watching."

"I suppose that's true," said Wofford, flipping the butt of his cigarette into the fire, "but there is one thing that a hanging does make certain; the hanged one's lawless days are finished."

At first light as they saddled their game, hearty horses, a clattering noise burst upon them.

In Tyrone's mind flashed the memory of the firecrackers of a Chinese New Year in New York City—snippety-snippety-snippety, poppity-pop-pop—racketing through the canyon.

"Ambush!" cried Wofford.

Hell yes, that's gunfire, realized Tyrone; how could there be Chinese firecrackers in Palo Duro Canyon?

Like rain, bullets drummed and pock'd the ground, stung trees and, a torrent now, flicked and churned the surface of the river behind him.

The sound was like swarming bees.

Bullets buzz, Tyrone's mind recorded. Readers of the books of Beadle and Adams take note: bullets buzz!

Wofford was shouting. "Cover, cover."

Tyrone scrambled down, belly-sliding toward a hump-back rock.

Ping, ping, ping, said the ricocheting bullets.

Buzz, buzz, buzz; ping, ping, ping; buzzzz!

STING!

The bullet felt like the bite of a yellow-jacket, he thought as his head snapped back; a puppet's being yanked by a string.

For an instant, his whole body tingled. Then cold swept through, ice in his blood, and he had a fleeting impression that he was ten years old again and hit with a snowball that was more mud off the street than ice.

His mouth tasted like metal.

He felt drunk, worse than after a night's carousing in McGlory's Garden of Eden. Numbness rose in him like the stroke of a woman with cool hands.

Limp as a rag doll, he dropped behind the rock, flat on the ground, out like a light.

Presently, he jerked awake.

How long he'd been out he would never know.

Seconds? Minutes? An hour?

Neither that day nor years later, looking back, could he say for sure how much time had passed.

Sitting up, he shook his head and raised a hand to his forehead to wipe away a trickle of moisture—he thought it was water where the snowball had hit him—but when he looked at his palm he gaped in amazement at a wide smear of blood.

Groggily, he thought, Some bastard put a rock in that goddamned snowball!

Reality seeped back.

This isn't a New York street, a voice inside him screamed. This is Texas.

Palo Duro Canyon!

It wasn't a snowball that hit him; it was a bullet.

So this is what it's like to be shot, he thought, raising his hand again and tenderly touching the shallow crease of the wound on the right side of his forehead.

He thought, If I can move my hand, I'm alive.

The bees were gone.

The river-rush filled his ears.

A horse neighed; Redskin's voice.

He always was a talker, Tyrone thought.

What was it that spared him, he wondered as he pushed himself to his feet, a spent bullet or his hard noggin?

"You got the hard head of the Irish!" his father had screamed at him once. His father had been as quick to hit him as he was to slam his wife.

"It'll take more than that to kill this Irishman," said that cruel man's son now, laughingly, as he staggered to his feet.

He turned looking for Wofford.

The laughter turned to a gagging lump in his throat.

Three bullets had ripped the chest. Another tore through the right arm. A fifth was dead-center in his back.

There was no telling how many had hit before he died, but one thing was plain. He'd gone out fighting. The gun lying at his fingertips had been emptied.

THIRTY-ONE

Tascosa

Long before it got the name Tascosa, the juncture of three small creeks and the Canadian River had been on the map as a crossroads of a pair of trails. One was the Spanish Road from west to east along the Canadian. The other was the buffalo route, south to north. Both took advantage of the spot's low banks and shallow water that was free of quicksand. Comanches following the buffalo had found the place to their liking, as did Mexican *comancheros* who stayed to trade with them despite occasional raids of pillaging and scalpings. In springtime because of floods created by the runoff of melting winter snows, the land was lush with grass and wildlife, including wild turkey, antelope, bears and elk, and the rich soil was fine for raising fruits and vegetables and keeping domesticated animals.

Scores of miles from the nearest law, the clannish people who settled there led hard, disappointing lives, turning wary and guarded eyes toward everyone who wasn't like them and offering a safe haven to many who were fleeing authority, as so many of them had, hurrying up the Spanish Trail from whatever troubles had threatened them in the arid towns of Mexico or Taos or Santa Fe in New Mexico.

Early among them had been the Borregos family of Taos who'd come looking for a place like that which their ancestors had known in Spain where they could raise sheep and goats, found it beside the generous Canadian River and established a settlement called Plazito Borregos. It was they who assayed the wet, lush land and named it Atascosa, which means "boggy."

A family named Martinez came. The Gurules brothers. Casimero Romero, of Castilian ancestry, settled, arriving in luxury with a coach and fourteen prairie schooners.

A few years later, the large Saldana family had drifted over from Santa Fe. A standoffish group, they boasted numerous cousins.

Many of the Saldanas, the people of Tascosa learned, ruefully, were wanted for crimes from whence they'd emigrated, but none could claim the notoriety of two of the eldest—Refugio Ruiz Saldana and his second-cousin, Sostenes. A thief and murderer, Sostenes had shown no trace of redeeming social value since the age of eight. Rawboned and six-feet-two at age 35, he was black-bearded and barrel-chested with a broad seat and thick thighs, requiring a tall and broad-chested horse, which he claimed to have ridden into battle beside Porfirio Diaz. Those who knew him well believed that Diaz would have strung him up rather than claim him as a compatriot. He wore a brace of pistols and a pair of bandoliers across his chest. He lived in a two-room adobe a mile west of the town.

His cousin had been his guest for two days.

Arriving in the dead of night, Saldana had declared, "I'm on the run from the Rangers, *amigo!*"

"How many?" roared Sostenes.

"Dunno. Maybe a whole comp'ny. Twenty. Thirty. I ain't seen 'em but I know they's behind me, led by one named Wofford who's been gunnin' for me a long time.

They raided Hezekiah. Wiped it out five, six days ago. I been ridin' since."

"No problem," said Sostenes confidently. "In the mornin' we'll round up some men and scatter 'em around to be lookouts. Anybody comes close to Tascosa what don't belong here, we'll know about it."

"Two riders," was the report the next evening. "Makin' camp in the Palo Duro." The messenger was a boy, breathing hard.

"Where in the Duro?" demanded Saldana.

"Foot of the Indian trail, east of Canyon. You know the place."

"I sure do," blared Saldana.

An hour later, belly-down on the lip of the canyon and peering through field glasses, he whispered, "It's Wofford all right. And that skunk Tyrone!"

"Just the two?" said Sostenes.

"Yep."

"Too dark now," judged Sostenes. "We get them at sunup."

At first light, the firing began.

Tyrone, Saldana observed with grinning satisfaction, fell at once, dropping onto his face and not moving. *"Venganza!"* he muttered. *"Venganza,* pig."

Wofford returned fire, emptying his pistol.

Useless at that distance, Saldana thought, giggling gleefully as he watched rifles cut him down.

"We go down and make sure they're dead," said Sostenes.

"They're finished," grunted Saldana. "Leave 'em for the buzzards."

THIRTY-TWO

The Texas Ranger

Under a tall cottonwood he'd picked out as a landmark, Tyrone fashioned a makeshift burial, wrapping Wofford in his blanket, duster coat and slicker and covering his head with his saddle, then piling on stones, fallen tree branches, brush and leaves.

He would come back, he vowed, bringing shovels for the digging of a proper grave and accompanied by Rangers who would fire a fitting volley with brand-new Winchesters in tribute and a preacher to speak a prayer.

He supposed he ought to say something now.

But what? he wondered, taking off his hat.

A string of adjectives came to mind: brave, fearless, tireless, dauntless, top rider, sharp tracker, expert shot, reliable friend.

All that could be lumped into a single prayer, he decided.

Bowing his head, he said, "Lord, here lies a Texas Ranger."

Fittingly, the sky was a mournful gray and weeping a cold mist as he rode out of the north end of the canyon on Redskin with Wofford's horse tethered behind,

Wofford's Winchester sheathed and cinched to Redskin's cold-stiff and creaking saddle and Wofford's Colt tucked under his own gunbelt. In a wallet under his shirt he carried Wofford's star-shaped badge.

By the time he'd climbed to the plateau, the rain was heavy and when he rode into the clustered shacks, trading post and saloon that called themselves the town of Canyon at the tip of Palo Duro it had turned into a windblown torrent that swept under the saloon's shingled porch roof and puddled in the warps of the worn plank flooring in front of the yellow-painted door.

There were no horses at the hitching rail.

Except for a plump woman behind a bar built to accommodate half a dozen drinkers, the dimly-lit, tobacco smoke-scented saloon was unpopulated. Opposite the bar were three round tables circled by straight-back chairs with cane seats. Signs advertising beer and whiskey brands speckled white plastered walls tinted cigar-and-cigarette-smoke yellowish.

"Some weather," he declared, pausing inside the door and shaking water out of his poncho and hat.

"Be glad it ain't snow," said the woman. Polishing the top of the stubbiest bar he'd ever encountered, she was a momentary picture of his mother mopping the kitchen table—slightly slope-shouldered and bent with thick, flabby, motherly arms and a generous bosom forming drooping calico arcs at the top of a white apron. "A shade colder, this'd be a right respectable blizzard and you'd be stuck here half the winter," she added, coming up straight to look at him across the room, sizing him up, fearlessly. "This could turn into snow yet. Maybe a couple of feet."

"Being snowed in might not be so bad, providin' the liquor held out and the women were friendly," he said with a wink. "You happen to serve mescal?" he asked, bellying the bar.

"Does a dog have fleas?"

"How far to Amarillo?" he asked while she did a little

curtsy to fetch a bottle from below the bar. That Tascosa was his goal seemed better not said, he figured. "Might Amarillo be close enough to get there by noon?"

"Twelve miles north and a trifle east," she said, pouring his drink. "What's the hurry? Nothin' there I ever heard about that's worth drownin' for to get to it. Last I heard it was nothin' but a bunch of mud huts belongin' to buffalo skinners. What's a good-lookin' galoot like you want in that dump?"

"Man promised me a job," he said boldly, finding the lying easy. "I'm supposed to meet him there at noon today. Don't want to lose a new job by being late. Will this road that I'm on take me there?"

"It forks a ways up. Take the right-hand. T'other goes to Tascosa. No jobs there, believe me. Unless you have a hankerin' to chase sheep."

He looked toward a rain-washed window and the grayness beyond. "Think this godawful weather'll let up anytime soon?"

"Not likely afore noon."

"Well, doesn't matter, I suppose," he said, slapping down the price of the mescal. "I can't get any wetter than I am."

"Yeah, you do look like a half-drowned pup," she chuckled, scooping up his coin. "If you're hungry, I can whip up some bacon and eggs. A cuppa hot coffee wouldn't take that long, neither."

Sorely tempted, he hesitated, but the memory of Wofford's fresh grave and an appetite for revenge was stronger than the appeal of a decent breakfast. "Better not if I want to make Amarillo by noontime," he said, adhering to the lie about his true destination, although lying to this decent woman gnawed at his conscience.

"You go careful, son," she said as he turned toward the door. "This is rough territory for goin' it alone—Injuns and bandits and men on the run from the law. A gang of 'em rode through here just this mornin', headin' same way as you."

"A gang, eh?" he said, urgently. "How many?"

"About six, led by a Tascosa ne'er do well name of Sostenes and another bad penny, a cousin of his name of Saldana," she said with digust. "I thought he was gone forever and glad of it, but appears he's back. Keep in mind that they're a nest of rattlers should you run across 'em. Wouldn't want to see you killed." She picked up his glass and wiped it out with the corner of her apron. "There's too few good-lookin' men around here as it is."

"Appreciate the sentiment," he said, smiling and putting on his soaked hat.

Half an hour later in the unrelenting downpour he came to the fork in the rain-filling rutted road. At its point stood a wooden post supporting a pair of boards crudely axed into opposing arrows, the right lettered A M E R I L L O and the left, slightly slanted toward the ground and punctuated by a bullet hole, declaring: T A S C O S A, 30 MILES.

"Not very far now, Red," he said, gently stroking the plucky horse's slick, steamy neck and reining him into a wagon trail that ran straight toward the murky horizon across the treeless plain, noting that whatever tracks Saldana and his gang may have left after thundering through Canyon that morning, if they'd come this way, had been obliterated by the incessant rain.

THIRTY-THREE

Sign of the Ram

Fronted by a plank walk under a steeply pitched roof of weathered shingles, the saloon faced the muddy street with a two-story false front. Hanging from it and swaying in the wind was a sign painted with the defiant profile and daunting coiled horns from which the flat-topped, clapboard-sided Ram's Head took its name.

Behind a solid wooden door with a metal, tongued latch, a piano was thumping a Mexican beat.

At the hitching post stood a pair of large horses.

The first as Tyrone rode up was a blocky chestnut. Plainly rigged, it was saddled for an ample seat. In a scabbard slung from it was a Sharp's rifle.

Beyond the chestnut, impatiently pawing the mud, was a familiar, big dappled gray with a rain-slicked, silver-studded black saddle with a matching holster sheathing a gleaming Winchester '73.

Kneeling in the mud beside the gray, he lifted the right hind foot. Thumbing away flakes of mud, he cleaned the shoe. "You got a nail missing, big fella," he said, letting go of the foot. Rising, he patted the horse's wet rump. "I guess I'd better let your owner know about it, hunh?"

The rain was a cold mist, the wind gusty from the northwest and the ground mushy as he led Redskin and Wofford's horse to the protected southeast side of the saloon.

Leaning against the windowless wall, he felt the banging of the piano through the boards. Catfooting, he moved to the rear. Peering cautiously around the corner, he found sloping ground leading to a distant line of trees that marked the south bank of the Canadian River, a small stable, a ramshackle woodshed with beer barrels piled against it, the crumbling ruin of a prairie schooner whose lopsided wheels offered cross-eyed evidence of a broken axle and a yellow, trim two-seater privy with a sagging twin-planked boardwalk connecting it to the back door of the saloon.

Easing toward the door, he found himself beneath a narrow, chin-high window. Through its rain-streaked grime, he looked directly into the saloon.

Along the wall to his left ran the bar. Behind it stood a stubby bartender with a prim waxed black mustache and engaged in the never-ending task of keepers of bars, swabbing the bar top and keeping tabs on the levels of liquor in the glasses of the elbow-leaning clientele. Unfamiliar to Tyrone, two of these were pistol-bearing. Leaning sidewise at the far end and facing one another, they were engaged in the never-ending pastime of saloon patrons—jawing, as it was called in McGlory's Garden of Eden, augurin' in the cowboy resorts of the West.

Of six square tables occupying the right side of the long smoke-fogged room, four were unoccupied.

Three poker players with holstered sidearms huddled over their cards at the fifth next to the piano player, a slender youth, unarmed.

Nearest to the front door, the last was claimed by two large men. Seated side by side with three pistols within easy reach before them, they had their backs to the rear of the room and its small window, but even from behind there was no mistaking Saldana.

Obviously the owner of two of the guns, the second man's bear-like chest was crisscrossed with a bullet-studded bandolier. Broad hips were girdled by two gun-belts draped with hogleg holsters. Was this Sostenes, Saldana's cousin? Tyrone wondered. Had this mountain of a man been with Saldana at the Palo Duro? Had bullets from his pistols and rifle buzzed down from the bluffs? Was he as guilty as Saldana? Did his name appear in Wofford's Book of Knaves? Did it matter, really? Obviously, there was going to be no coming to grips with Saldana without having to deal with the man with him, whatever his name, whatever his connection to Saldana.

And what of the others? Might the auguring pair by the door figure in? The boy banging the piano? The poker players? The bartender? Were they all part of Saldana's gang? Or would they, faced with guns, scramble for cover?

Would he find himself going up against a saloon bristling with drawn guns? he wondered as he slipped away from the window. Could he be the match of the lone Ranger of Wofford's last, bragging tale? Was he the equal of the one daring Ranger sent to quell a riot single-handedly?

A reporter's timeless questions assaulted him as he slipped to the side of the building.

Where?

In the saloon? The street?

How?

Barging in with drawn guns and demanding Saldana's immediate surrender? Lying in wait until he emerged toward his big horse out front? Challenging him in the middle of Tascosa's boggy street? Catch him with his pants down in the privy out back?

That idea tickled.

Snow fell.

Light flakes, they soon dusted the ground.

He looked skyward. Cold flakes settled on his nose; a kiss.

Flattening himself against the side wall, he sucked in breath.

When?

"No time like the present," he muttered.

Seeing him as he rounded the front of the saloon, Redskin nodded his head impatiently.

"Soon, fella," Tyrone whispered. "One way or another, it'll be over soon."

When he stepped onto the porch, the planks squeaked.

Jerking its head, Saldana's big gray neighed.

The wind rose, gusting beneath the roof and swirling wisps of snow into a dance in a sliver of light seeping beneath the closed door.

Sidling next to it from the right, Tyrone drew his Colt into his right hand and reached with his left to the metal latch, depressing the cold curl of its dog-like tongue.

Sprung loose, the door drifted open a crack.

Swinging round, he kicked it open.

THIRTY-FOUR

Snowbound

"Texas Ranger!"

Half-crouched, Tyrone held his pistol in steady accordance with Morgan's Catechism of the Gun, hands clasped at the point of the triangle of his rigid arms, looking down the barrel of the Colt and fixing Saldana in the sight.

"Nobody move!"

For an instant, the big, dim, smoky room was a tintype photograph.

The auguring pair nearest him were frozen with their mouths open and their six-guns sheathed. The bartender stood in place as if he and his mopping rag were glued. The three poker players were sitting pat, their holdings pressed close to their chests. With gracefully curved fingers and uplifted hands, the piano player hung suspended between the tinny notes of an unfinished tune. The bandolier-chested bear of a man beside Saldana gaped. Stunned with surprise, Saldana was staring slack-jawed.

"The jig's up, Sally!" declared Tyrone. "I'm arresting you on warrants for murder and other crimes and misdemeanors."

Saldana's jaw flickered into motion. The thick cords of

veins in his bull neck throbbed. The mouth twisted mockingly. He snorted a laugh. "Is that . . . right?"

"Indeed it is."

"Go to hell," snarled the bear-chested man to Saldana's right, thrusting meaty hands toward the guns lying between them on the table, but as they clutched the grips of two pistols and started coming up, Tyrone swung the triangle of his arms a trace, firing once.

As abruptly as the saloon had become immobile with his kicking open of the door, it reacted to the explosion of his Colt with scrambling animation. The pair of augurers sank out of the plane of fire. The bartender ducked behind the bar. The card players flung themselves under tables. The piano player hunkered beneath the overhanging keyboard.

Drilled an inch above the X formed by his bandoliers, Sostenes clutched at his chest, but the movement was involuntary, the twitching clutch of a man with a .44 bullet punching into his chest, passing through the heart and exploding out his back with a force sufficient to tip him and his chair and tumble them racketing backward into the wall and a slow sliding to the sawdusted floor.

In the moment that it took his cousin to die, Saldana was also in motion, whisking his gun from the table, rolling sideways from his chair and into a crouching lurch toward the rear door. Leaping outside, he dashed for the cover of the ruined wagon, spun round and fired once at the door, splintering the wood above the pullstring latch.

Jerking the door open, Tyrone dove out, hitting the ground and rolling right and picking up a crusting of snow. It was nearly an inch deep now and thickening fast, whipped by gusts of whistling wind. Flat on his belly, he fired at a shadow behind the wagon, but the thumping run of boots signalled a miss.

Saldana fired one retreating shot from behind the privy.

Answering it, Tyrone missed again.

Running sounds receded down the slope toward the river.

Rising and dashing past the privy, Tyrone zigzagged toward the woodshed and out of the corner of his eye caught a muzzle flash that was an orange tongue against the black shadow of brush far down the hill.

As he slammed against the woodshed, the bullet ping'd a hanging bucket an inch above his head.

In a wild serpentine sprint, he hurtled down the slope, firing twice with no expectation of a hit; covering fire. Plunging into a thicket already piling up with drifted snow, he heard a shot but could not see where it came from.

It slammed into his right arm. Striking an inch below the shoulder, it spun him like a top and when he hit the ground, he rolled over and over until stopped by underbrush.

Seething with anger and somehow—miraculously—still clutching his gun, he fired blindly until the hammer hit with a cold, lifeless click.

Then came wrenching, searing pain. His hand trembled violently, protesting the weight of the Colt.

The river was close, rippling, swift and turgid. The wind howled in the trees, barely visible through the raging snow, a blizzard now. Breathing hard, he lay still, waiting and listening.

Presently, Saldana's voice cut through. "Gotcha, didn't I, kid? Plugged you as clean as a bird on the wing!"

Feeling faint, Tyrone groped in the snow for his gun.

"Shot your bolt, ain'tcha?" bellowed Saldana. "Emptied out your gun. The one inside, the one by the privy, four just now. Six in all. That's the lot for you. But I got two left, don't I? And lots more in my belt. And I ain't got no slugs in me, do I? Think you can reload that gun of yours with only one good arm? I don't think so! I think you're finished, kid! Yeah, you've cashed all your chips."

Reaching desperately for his gun, Tyrone felt a spasm

of pain worse than before, squeezing like a vise. Blood glued his shirt to his skin. His stomach churned sourly. His head swam. He feared he was going to pass out.

Saldana bellowed again, tauntingly. "It's you who's flat on his ass and bleedin' in the snow and out of ammunition, ain't it? And too shot up and weak to do a damn thing, 'cept die like a dog in this storm. What shall I do, kid? Let you lay there with the life bein' sapped out of you by the bleedin' and the freezin'? Or do you want me to do you a favor and end your sufferin' by blowin' your head off?"

Fighting the crushing pain, Tyrone rolled onto his useless right arm and drew Wofford's pistol with his left hand.

"Hey kid?" shouted Saldana. "You really hurt, huh? Make a noise! Let me hear where you are. I'll come over there and put you out of your misery."

With shivering-cold fingers, Tyrone gripped Wofford's heavy gun. Damned hogleg, he thought. Thing weighs half a ton and all I got is one hand! And the left hand at that! So much for Morgan's two-handed stance.

"Where are ya, kid?" shouted Saldana. He was closer now, advancing slowly from the river. "Hey, kid, you still alive?"

"Still breathin', Sally," he yelled, covering the sound of the click as he cocked the cold, stiff gun with a stiff, cold thumb.

"But just barely, eh?" grunted Saldana. "Well don't fret, kid, 'cause your sufferin's just about over at last. Fact is, I figured we got you when we got that Ranger you were with. My cousin wanted to ride down and check to be sure. Guess I shoulda took his advice. He'd be alive now, 'stead of dead inside, thanks to you. Who the devil are you, anyway? What brought you around lookin' to make trouble for me? I don't recall I ever did anythin' agin' you. What put a hair across your ass concernin' me?"

"I figured somebody ought to teach you proper respect for a lady."

"What lady?"

"Evangeline!" Tyrone gasped.

Saldana's answering laugh was the howl of a coyote. "Why, she's nothin' but a whore! You done all this on her account?"

"That was it, till Palo Duro."

"Now it's *venganza,* eh? It's a damned chilly night for revenge, no matter how sweet its appeal may be."

"It's a dish best served cold."

"Cold's what you'll be in a second, kid. Cold, dead meat."

"You're enjoying this! Cat and mouse. Tormenting people's a kick for you, right?"

Saldana fell silent but the silence itself was the answer to the question, thought Tyrone as he squinted against the sting of the obscuring wind-driven snow, searching for any sign of him. He'd been advancing cautiously but, judging by the direction of his voice, straight.

"I'm a Texas Ranger now, by the way," shouted Tyrone, hoping to coax a rise. "Thanks to you."

Saldana snorted a laugh, very close. "Soon to be a dead one."

"There's plenty more. One of them'll get you, sooner or later."

"Well, it ain't gonna be you," cried Saldana.

Jumping up from the brush directly ahead, he formed a looming silhouette against the snow that was as black as a paper cut-out target.

"Go for the gut," whispered Tyrone, reciting Morgan's first rule of the Catechism of the Gun, and squeezing Wofford's trigger.

The snow which soon covered Saldana's corpse also quickly covered the dripped blood which marked Tyrone's staggering trail up from the river to the front of the Ram's Head Saloon where Redskin waited patiently with Wofford's horse, both having collected a white coat.

Whatever inclination to pursue and punish him that may have flourished among the patrons of the saloon or within the clannish residents of Tascosa had declined quickly before the brunt of the blizzard. That the Ranger would perish in the storm, no one doubted.

But he did not perish.

Looking back on that fierce night, Tyrone would attribute his survival to the fact that he seemed to have found fresh strength even as he was riding out of Tascosa, to the courage of his remarkable horse, to having the wind at his back and to a lull in the blizzard that lasted for nearly an hour, long enough for him to reach the town of Canyon where a woman who reminded him of his mother ran the saloon.

"Good lord, you look half froze," she exclaimed as he stumbled in. "And my word, you've been shot!"

"Sorry for the inconvenience, ma'am," he said weakly.

"Lord prevent the day when I look on havin' a good-lookin' man around as an inconvenience!"

"I promise I'll move on as soon as the weather clears."

"This is the Staked Plains in winter, son," she said. "Next good weather we'll see is prob'ly months away!"

With that, he collapsed, beginning weeks of recovery from his wound whose end would be marked by him asking the woman who had nursed him as tenderly as if she were his own mother, "Would you happen to have some writing paper?"

EPILOGUE

A Letter from Texas

The azure sky of a peerless afternoon arched above Madison Square on the first of June 1876 as Tyrone's four-wheel carriage crossed Twenty-third Street and drew up before the splendid columned portico of the stately entrance to the Fifth Avenue Hotel. Beyond it stretched the grand entrance hall, running 160 feet in length, 27 wide and 15 high, scattered with plumply upholstered sofas and its marble floor covered with plush red carpeting. Striding through, he passed the gleaming doors of a quiet sitting room known as the "Amen Corner" where deals were hatched by political bosses and ratified by their sycophants. In the luxurious suites above, the celebrated of the world were frequent guests and many of the rich and successful of New York maintained residences. Tyrone had been living here for six months, riding the crest of the phenomenal sales of *Showdown in Hell Town* and *I Rode with the Texas Rangers.*

"Good day, Mr. Tyrone," beamed the hotel manager as Tyrone approached the desk. "Your mail, sir," he said, drawing a single letter from a pigeon hole. "It was forwarded to you by your publishers."

Dated by the post office in Houston, Texas, three weeks ago, it bore the imprint MMM Ranch, Goliad.

"It's from Morgan," he exclaimed, tearing it open and rushing to a sofa to read it.

Dear Tyrone,

I write in care of your publishers, Beadle and Adams, trusting that this will be forwarded by them and that it finds you enjoying good health and fortune.

Thanks to the generosity of Shanghai Pierce who obtained them on a visit to Chicago, I am in receipt of copies of your books, which I have now read, enjoying them immensely.

I write to compliment you and to relate a recent event which concerned McNelly's Rangers and King Fisher, bringing that notorious individual to account, at last, for his misdeeds.

Following several daring attacks upon the Cortinista gangs, during which more than a dozen of the scoundrels were killed, McNelly concentrated his efforts on the Fisher gang, taking the "King" by surprise at his Pendencia headquarters.

According to reports reaching me here in Goliad, that moment was quite dramatic as Fisher emerged from his house to confront McNelly himself. Picture it with your author's eye! Right there, facing one another at not more than five paces, were by long odds the two best pistol fighters in Texas.

Although I expect that you might have written the scene as one of terrible violence, I am happy to note that the entire matter was settled without gunplay. I am told that both men simply smiled at each other and that Fisher meekly handed his guns to the captain, who said, "We had you."

"Yes, you had me," Fisher replied. "Pretty neat."

Pretty neat, indeed! For McNelly had, at last, arrested the biggest name on the Mexican border!

I wish that were the end of the story. Alas, it is not, for Fisher managed to slip from the snare through various legal technicalities and was released after a hearing before a judge in Eagle Pass. Nonetheless, McNelly delivered a stern lecture to him, warning Fisher to get out of the outlawing business. "You could make a good citizen," he told him, "but you'd also make a nice corpse. All outlaws look good dead."

So, King Fisher remains at large, but I am not by any means dismayed, for I sense a change in the air. The law has come to the chapparal and I believe it is here to stay.

I am worried about McNelly, however. His health, which had never been good, has taken a turn for the worse. I do not believe he has many years left to live. When that sad day of his death comes, he surely will be recorded in the annals of Texas as a genuine hero.

"A hero, indeed," muttered Tyrone, looking up from Morgan's letter at the buzzing bustle of the grand hotel's glorious gallery and remembering the admiring look that always came over Andy Wofford's face whenever he'd spoken of McNelly.

He thought back to his days at the Pendencia, smiling slightly as he recalled King Fisher's proud struttings, unable to think of Fisher without feeling some understanding of his appeal to the people of the Nueces Strip to whom he was a Rio Grande Robin Hood. Perhaps, he thought, the King would take McNelly's stern lecture to heart, mend his ways and leave a positive mark on Texas.

Morgan's letter continued:

On a personal note, I have sad news to relate regarding my wife, Rebecca, who passed away as the result of a fall while riding her favorite horse.

The future of the Colter ranch is now in my hands and I have great expectations that it will become one of the most important cattle ranches in the state.

After a suitable period of mourning, I married again, mainly for the benefit of my son Colt, and now he has been presented with a brother.

In their honor, I have changed the name of the ranch, calling it the Triple M.

I hope you will honor us with a visit very soon.

Yours sincerely,
MORGAN

Carefully folding the letter into the pocket of his coat, Tyrone went to his suite where his writing desk overlooked the crowded streets and sidewalks of the heart of Manhattan, so far from the boundlessness of the prairies of Kansas and Texas that all that he had experienced there might have seemed a dream, save for his two books and the letter from Morgan in his pocket.

On a sheet of hotel foolscap, he began writing.

My dear Morgan,

Your letter has been gratefully but sadly received and I am pleased to acknowledge your generous invitation to visit you and your sons at Goliad and will try to do so.

I have been giving serious consideration to returning to the West to begin work on a new book about a gang of robbers who've been running wild from Texas to Missouri.

My publishers are after me to track them down and get their stories.

Perhaps you've heard of them—the James brothers.